# EVERYTHING YOU NEED TO KNOW ABOUT NIGHTMARES! AND HOW TO DEFEAT THEM

# Books by Jason Segel and Kirsten Miller

*Nightmares!*

*Nightmares! The Sleepwalker Tonic*

*Nightmares! The Lost Lullaby*

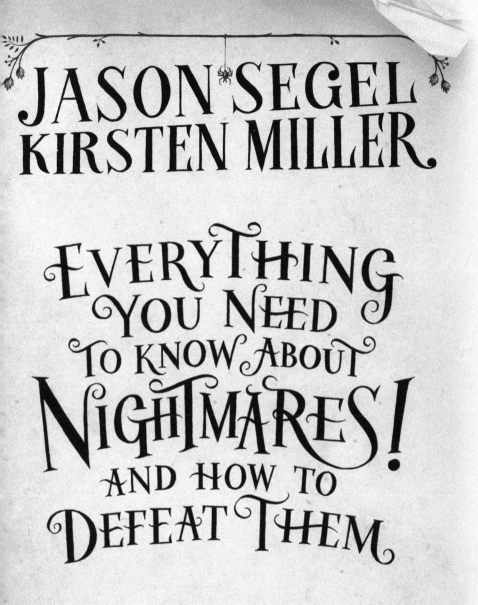

# JASON SEGEL
# KIRSTEN MILLER

# EVERYTHING YOU NEED TO KNOW ABOUT NIGHTMARES! AND HOW TO DEFEAT THEM

~ ILLUSTRATED BY KARL KWASNY ~

DELACORTE PRESS

Copyright © 2017 by The Jason Segel Company
Illustrations by Karl Kwasny with illustration assistant Stephanie Pepper

All rights reserved. Published in the United States by Delacorte Press, an imprint of Random House Children's Books, a division of Penguin Random House LLC, New York.

Delacorte Press is a registered trademark and the colophon is a trademark of Penguin Random House LLC.

Visit us on the Web! randomhousekids.com
Educators and librarians, for a variety of teaching tools, visit us at RHTeachersLibrarians.com

Library of Congress Cataloging-in-Publication Data
is available upon request.

ISBN 978-0-385-74431-7 (hc) — ISBN 978-0-375-99160-8 (lib. bdg.)
ISBN 978-0-385-38406-3 (ebook)

The text of this book is set in 12.2-point Sabon MT.
Interior design by Stephanie Moss

Printed in the United States of America
10 9 8 7 6 5 4 3 2 1
First Edition

*To Sharon Jackson,*
*my partner on this journey.*
*Thank you.*
*Love,*
*JS*

# CONTENTS

# THE TRUTH ABOUT NIGHTMARES

Each evening when we fall asleep, our minds embark on a journey. If we're lucky, we make our way to the Dream Realm, a wonderful world where we're able to live out our fondest fantasies—like riding a unicorn, scoring the winning goal at the World Cup, or sneaking into a cheese shop after dark. But more often than we'd like, we close our eyes and find ourselves trapped in a sinister world filled with Werewolves and Giant Scaly Things and everything else that goes bump in the night.

This is the Netherworld, the land of Nightmares. We all visit the Netherworld countless times in our lives—and by now you've probably learned that it isn't always easy to leave. Night after night, you may find yourself being chased or gobbled or stalked by creatures that seem determined to scare you. The bad news is these Nightmares are every bit as real as you and me. Fortunately, there's some good news too. No matter how gruesome they are, Nightmares can't hurt us—and they don't want to either. When they make you shiver, scream, or wet your bed, they're only doing their jobs.

You see, Nightmares force us to face our fears. Everyone is scared of *something*. (We could personally list a *hundred* things.) The Netherworld is where our fears come to life. When you see them, your first instinct is to flee. But that would be a *big* mistake. You can't run away from a Nightmare. You might manage to escape one night, but your fears will be back to taunt you the next time you fall asleep.

As terrible as this sounds, there's no need to despair. Even the worst Nightmares can be beaten—you just need a little grit, some cleverness, and the courage to stand your ground. If you face your Nightmares—if you don't run away—you can find a way to make them vanish for good.

This handbook will give you all the advice you need to beat the most common species of Nightmares. You'll learn about their strengths, weaknesses, and quirks. With this book by your bedside, you can rest assured that you're totally prepared for your next trip to the Netherworld.

## Good night, and good luck!

# LURKERS AND STALKERS

Lurkers and Stalkers are some of the Netherworld's creepiest residents. Unlike other species of Nightmares, they're rarely seen. The trouble is, they can always see *you*.

Lurkers and Stalkers like to hide in dense forests, at the bottom of large bodies of water (lakes, oceans, Olympic-size swimming pools), or in dimly lit metropolitan areas. Masters of disguise, they can blend into any background. Lurkers will usually watch you from a distance, while Stalkers prefer to follow you. The good news is, neither group is dangerous. They (almost) never attack. They prefer a slow, steady scare. Nightmares starring Lurkers and Stalkers have been known to drag on for days.

# PRO TIP!

You don't need to *see* Lurkers or Stalkers to know they're nearby! Look for these warning signs.

- ◆ Cold, clammy hands
- ◆ Hair standing up on the back of your neck
- ◆ Extra-large goose bumps (spider bite–size)

If you're suffering from one or more of these symptoms, there's probably a Lurker or Stalker around!

# THE THING IN THE WOODS

You don't know what it is, but you know it's out there. Maybe you see yellow eyes glowing in the dark, or hear something prowling among the trees. Or perhaps you catch the unmistakable scent of mushrooms, rotting leaves, and terrible BO. If so, you're dreaming about the Thing in the Woods (TITW).

The star of countless camping-themed nightmares, the Thing has tortured every city kid who's ever gone to summer camp in the country. Call it a monster. Call it a beast. Just don't call it Bigfoot. Its feelings get hurt when it's confused with its famous neighbor.

Nightmares about the Thing in the Woods are common when people are expecting big life changes. If you're about to start a new grade at school, move to another town, go to prison, or set off on an expedition along the Amazon River, you may soon find yourself dreaming about the Thing.

Nothing's more frightening than the unknown (whether it's the future or whatever's under your bed right now). But hiding from things you can't see doesn't work. In the case of Lurkers like the Thing in the Woods, you should take immediate action. Don't cower, and don't run away. Find a flashlight and go out and greet it. (Consider bringing a s'more or two in case your Thing is hungry.) As soon as you can see it, you'll probably realize that it's really not scary at all!

## STRENGTHS

- It knows the woods far better than you do.
- Unlike you, it can see perfectly well in the dark.
- You won't hear it unless it wants you to hear it.
- It can unzip a tent.

## WEAKNESSES

- The TITW may act tough, but it's really quite shy. It may run away the first time you introduce yourself.
- It can easily be bribed with s'mores, chocolate-covered granola bars, or burnt campfire marshmallows.

# Alfie Bluenthal and the Thing in the Woods

Alfie Bluenthal first spotted the Thing in the Woods at the end of May, about two weeks before he was due to head off to cooking camp for the summer. In his nightmare, Alfie was picking vegetables in his garden when he heard a beast panting in the woods at the edge of his backyard. He couldn't see the Thing, but it sounded big. And when he detected a horrible stench on the breeze, he knew anything that smelled *that* awful had to be *huge*.

Alfie ran into his house and slammed the door. But the panting didn't stop. It only grew louder. Soon he could hear the Thing on the other side of the door.

Alfie shouted for help, but his mom and dad didn't answer. (As parents in nightmares so often do, they'd abandoned their child to a terrible fate.) He rushed to his bedroom and pushed his bureau against the door, but he could still hear the panting—along with heavy footsteps in the hallway. Seconds after he'd crawled under the bed, he heard the bureau slowly sliding across the floor.

Alfie woke up from his nightmare before the Thing got him. And the very next morning, he paid a visit to the purple mansion. Charlie had an idea that he thought might help. "Your Thing sounds really hungry," he said. Alfie preferred the word *ravenous*. "Maybe you should stop running," Charlie advised, "and invite it over for dinner."

The following night, Alfie couldn't work up the courage to prepare a meal. After all, he was only just learning to cook. But the evening after that, he decided the nightmare needed to stop. Before he fell asleep, he found a recipe online that seemed easy to make, and when he got to the Netherworld, he felt completely prepared. In his nightmare, he whipped up a big batch of cacio e pepe. Then he set up a table in the backyard and waited for the Thing to arrive.

The delicious aroma of pasta and cheese lured his dinner guest out of the woods. As the beast slunk across Alfie's backyard toward the table, Alfie was amused to see that it was about the size of a toddler (though much furrier, and with an impressive set of teeth). Turned out the Nightmare's name was Bernard, and he and Alfie had a lot in common. They ate the pasta (which was absolutely delicious), talked about the latest advances in astrophysics, and discussed their summer plans.

The next night, Alfie cooked cacio e pepe for dinner in the Waking World, which blew his parents' minds. Then he went to sleep and dreamed of cooking camp. When he woke up, he couldn't wait for summer break to begin.

## CACIO E PEPE

### INGREDIENTS

- 1½ cups grated Romano cheese
- 1 cup grated Parmesan cheese
- 1 tablespoon black pepper
- salt
- ¾ pound dry spaghetti noodles
- olive oil

### INSTRUCTIONS

Dump the cheeses and pepper into a bowl and mix them together. Add some water a little at a time and stir until the mixture is as thick as glue.

Boil a big pot of salted water. Add the spaghetti.

Right before the pasta is completely cooked, use tongs to transfer it from the cooking pot to the bowl with cheese and pepper. Save a cup of the cooking water.

Stir the pasta, cheese, and pepper together. Add a little olive oil—and a little cooking water to make it creamy.

Eat and enjoy!!!

# OTHER "THINGS" YOU MIGHT MEET IN THE NETHERWORLD
## (AND WHAT TO HAVE ON HAND WHEN YOU DO!)

## The Thing in the Attic

Even if it's not frightening, it's probably pretty annoying. Things in the Attic tend to thump around quite a bit. Occasionally they'll thump so hard that they crash right through the ceiling. If you'd like to get rid of yours, try scattering a pocketful of acorns across the attic floor. The acorns will attract squirrels, and Things in the Attic *hate* squirrels. (They never developed a taste for them like the Thing in the Woods.) As soon as the furry little beasts move in, your Thing will move out. The only downside? You'll be left with a bunch of Netherworld squirrels, who aren't known to be particularly friendly.

## The Thing Right Behind You

It's so terrifying that you can't bring yourself to turn around. But you have to face it! That's where a small mirror comes in handy. Use your mirror to look the Thing Right Behind You in the eye and tell it to hit the road. Odds are, you won't have to say much more. The Thing will be so horrified by the sight of its own appearance that it will already have bolted.

## The Thing You Fear Most

Whatever it is—a giant millipede, the existential void, or Hickory Smoke Spam—you're sure to come across it in the Netherworld. To prepare for this meeting, you must be brave! Try imagining yourself standing face to face with your Nightmare. Now imagine reaching out and giving it a hug. (If your Nightmare is Spam, this could get pretty gross, but try it anyway.)

# SHADOWS

Shadows are by far the most common species of Stalker in the Netherworld. They're just about everywhere you look! Most of the time they play a supporting role in other bad dreams, helping to make those nightmares spookier and more atmospheric. Occasionally, however, a Shadow will become the star of the show. And when that happens, you better look out. ('Cause it's right behind you!)

Most Shadow Nightmares begin with the sensation that you're being followed—and you *are*. There's something creeping up on you, but when you spin around, nothing's there. All you can see is a strange patch of darkness on the ground. The truth is, you could be staring straight at a Shadow Nightmare and you'd never suspect a thing. Then, as soon as you're not looking, it'll reach out and stroke the nape of your neck, sending shivers down your spine. When you run, it will stay right on your heels. No matter how fast you book it, you'll never get away.

Here's what you need to know about Shadows: They don't want to hurt you. They *like* you! That's why they're always following you around. So think of your Shadow as your biggest fan—and try to get used to its company. Once a Shadow has found you, it's highly unlikely that you'll ever get rid of it for good. (But whenever you need a little alone time, all you have to do is turn on some lights.)

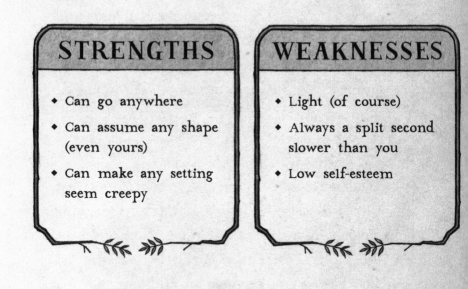

## STRENGTHS

- Can go anywhere
- Can assume any shape (even yours)
- Can make any setting seem creepy

## WEAKNESSES

- Light (of course)
- Always a split second slower than you
- Low self-esteem

SAD

Shadows are the children of the Netherworld's oldest Nightmare—the Dark. Try to imagine how hard that must be! Shadows know they'll never be as famous or as frightening as their world-renowned parent. Most are desperate to be something other than Shadows—they'd like nothing more than to be solid and real. That's why they're always taking the shapes of other objects!

## PRO TIP!

If a Shadow is behind you, for heaven's sake, don't run! The Nightmare will chase you wherever you go. It's best to continue at a slow pace and try to enjoy the Shadow's company. In fact, why not have a little chat with it? Your Shadow won't be able to talk back, but it will appreciate the effort. It's probably a good idea to get to know each other—you're going to be hanging out together for a while!

# THE BEASTS FROM BELOW

Commonly known as sea monsters (a name they truly despise), the Beasts from Below can be found in any large body of water. Classic Stalkers, they enjoy following ships, swimmers, and recreational water craft. Despite their terrifying appearance, they're playful and enjoy physical contact. They are known to bump rowboats, flip kayaks, and brush up against legs.

If you find yourself being stalked by a Beast from Below (BFB), there are several things you can do:

- **Sing it a song.** BFBs are suckers for sea shanties and classic Motown.

- **Avoid peeing in the water.** They hate that! And your Waking World mattress may suffer as well.

- **Hitch a ride.** (Note: It's important that you tell your BFB how long you can hold your breath.)

## STRENGTHS

- The element of surprise. BFBs are masters of timing and can pop out of the water when you least expect it.

- Many BFBs have long necks or tentacles, which are perfect for snatching people from boats with no warning.

## WEAKNESSES

- You have size on your side. You're not really big enough to be much of a snack.

- BFBs are not the largest creatures in the ocean. There are things down there that scare them to death too.

## FUN FACT!

Every Netherworld lake has its own Beast from Below. They're less common in the Waking World, but you can find them here too. (Just not in Scotland. The Loch Ness Monster is nothing but a silly legend.)

## PRO TIP!

If you expect to encounter a BFB, wear your swimsuit to bed. You might feel silly, but you'll be far more comfortable and your Nightmare will recognize (and respect) your preparedness!

# THE
# CHASERS

You know the feeling. There's something after you. You're running as fast as you can, but you can't seem to lose it. It's right on your heels—so close you can hear it panting or groaning or slurping the spit off its lips. You could be racing through a burnt-out city, a Romanian forest, or a Bed Bath & Beyond. It doesn't matter where you are or which kind of Chaser Nightmare is after you. If you stop, trip, or slow your pace, you're in serious trouble.

Chasers are among the Netherworld's most popular Nightmares. Some (such as saber-toothed tigers) have been around since human beings first began having bad dreams. Others regularly change their appearance to suit the latest trends.

If a Chaser is hounding you, there's a simple question you'll have to answer before you can shake it off: What the heck am I running from? As with all Nightmares, knowing what you're really scared of is half the battle!

Nightmares are your Waking World fears in disguise. And sometimes uncovering their true identities can take a little detective work.

**FUN FACT!**

Many people think Chasers and Gobblers belong to the same family of Nightmares. They do have many similarities, but there's one important difference. Chasers chase, but they don't always *catch*, and when they do, they rarely eat. Gobblers, on the other hand, may pursue you, but most would rather wait for you to fall into their traps. And once a Gobbler's got you, it will *always* chow down.

# PRO TIP!

Not sure what's after you? Here's a foolproof way to find out: simply lure your Nightmare into a booby trap! (A basic net trap usually works well.) Your aim is not to injure the beast, just to find out what it wants (some only want a little attention). Once you do, the chasing should stop immediately.

# ZOMBIES

It's important to remember that Zombies are people too. Sure, they may be falling apart, but underneath all that rotten flesh, they're just like you and me.

Don't take it too personally if the Netherworld's Walking Dead are after you and your brains. Zombies suffer from acute *hanger,* and the human brain just happens to be an excellent source of the vitamins and nutrients the Walking Dead crave. Fortunately, so is chopped liver.

The best way to avoid an attack is to prepare a big batch of chopped liver and slip it under your pillow before you drift off to sleep. (Vegetarians, take note: Cooking liver may be unpleasant, but when it comes to Zombies, a nice kale casserole will *not* do the trick. The authors of this chapter learned that the hard way.)

As soon as you're in the Netherworld, whip out your dish. Chopped liver should look and feel like brown Play-Doh, and if you have enough time before the Zombies attack, go ahead and get creative. Mold it into the shape of brains! They always appreciate the extra touch.

After your Zombies have eaten, you might be surprised by what pleasant company they are. Though it's probably a good idea to leave pretty soon after dinner. Those with bellies digest their food quickly, and you don't want to be around when it's time for their next meal.

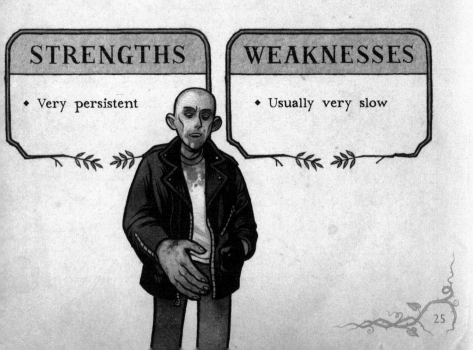

## STRENGTHS

- Very persistent

## WEAKNESSES

- Usually very slow

## Rocco and the Zombie (AKA Morgan)

Not long ago, Rocco Marquez went to sleep and found himself in the Netherworld's version of his hometown, Cypress Creek. The streets were deserted, dead leaves drifted in the evening wind, and the town was almost completely silent—aside from a strange shuffling sound coming from somewhere behind him.

Rocco slowly turned around, terrified of what he might see. Not far away, a Zombie was lumbering toward him. The dim glow of a streetlight revealed a man with a face that was missing at least two key features. Most sleepers would have screamed and run away. But the strange thing was, Rocco wasn't afraid of Zombies.

Rocco figured he'd gotten mixed up in someone else's nightmare, and rather than interfere, he decided to hit the road. Rocco was the fastest kid at Cypress Creek Elementary, so it didn't take much for him to leave the Zombie in the dust. But over the next few nights, he couldn't seem to shake it. Every night, Rocco would fall asleep and wake up in the Netherworld. Every night, he'd run from town. And every night, wherever he went, the Zombie was there, moaning and drooling as it tried to catch up with him.

After five straight nights in the Netherworld, Rocco had had enough. He wanted to get back to the Dream Realm, where he could spend his time playing soccer. So when he went to sleep the next night, Rocco set out to locate the Nightmare.

He discovered the Zombie waiting for him in his Netherworld backyard. He found out the Nightmare's name was Morgan, and aside from the smell, he was a pretty cool guy. Before he'd joined the Walking Dead, he'd been a professional soccer player. He wasn't interested in eating Rocco's brain (though he admitted the temptation was there). He just wanted to talk about sports with someone. So Rocco and the Zombie chatted about soccer all night. And the next time Rocco went to sleep, he did his new friend a favor: he brought the Zombie to the Dream Realm for the best soccer match either of them had ever played.

# WEREWOLVES

Everyone knows about Werewolves. And nearly everyone will meet a Werewolf Nightmare at some point. For centuries, the furry monsters have been in high demand in the Netherworld, and the attention has clearly gone to their heads. As a result, Werewolves can be conceited and unpleasant to be around—which makes them surprisingly easy to defeat.

As you know, Werewolves can only transform during a full moon. The rest of the month they live as ordinary humans and must conceal their identities. Back in the days when every peasant owned a pitchfork, Werewolves took great care to remain undercover. They bathed as soon as they returned from the woods and never bragged about their exploits at parties.

In modern times, however, Werewolves have become reckless. All it takes is some simple detective skills and you can easily hunt them down before the full moon comes out.

Werewolves hate it when anyone sees them changing from human to beast, so make sure your Werewolf knows you'll be watching during the next full moon—and capturing everything on camera. Rather than risk the embarrassment, they'll probably promise to leave you alone!

## STRENGTHS

- Highly advanced sense of smell
- Extremely fast reflexes
- Able to mingle with both humans and canines

## WEAKNESSES

- Dreadful oral hygiene
- Total attention hogs
- Scared of being spotted in the nude

## FUN FACT!

The easiest way to identify a Werewolf in human form is to sniff him or her out! Is there someone you've met in your Netherworld visits who reeks of wet, filthy dog? Or someone whose breath stinks like they just ate a raw deer? If so, you've found your villain.

## PRO TIP #1!

Before setting off into the woods, a Werewolf always hides a change of clothes nearby for when they return to human form. If you can find your Werewolf's secret stash, you'll have the ultimate bargaining tool.

## PRO TIP #2!

Werewolves are mesmerized by the full moon. They can't help but stop and howl whenever they see it. If you're being chased by a werewolf in your nightmare, make your way to a wide-open space where the moon is visible. That'll buy you a good minute or two of howl time to put a game plan together!

# WHAT TO DO

## A RAVENOUS BEAST IS CHASING YOU

Everyone agrees that being chased by a Ravenous Beast is a terrifying experience. But if you dream about the same one night after night, all that running and screaming can get kind of . . . tedious.

Let's be honest—a lot of Chasers aren't terribly intelligent. And some forget that their job as Nightmares is to help you face your fears. Over time, Chasers can become addicted to the thrill of pursuit, and they'll stay after you for days. The best way to beat these dim-witted Nightmares is to simply stop running. This, however, is not the recommended solution. There's always a small chance that the Chaser that's been after you for days is a Gobbler. And if you stop, you're going to be dinner. (Note: You can't die in the Netherworld, but getting eaten is still pretty awful.)

Fortunately, there are several safe and effective ways to get rid of an annoyingly persistent Ravenous Beast. Here are a couple we recommend:

- Run through a supermarket. (Many a Ravenous Beast has been ditched in the sausage section.) Food fairs and restaurant kitchens work just as well. School cafeterias, on the other hand, are unlikely to distract them.

- Lead your Nightmare into a perfume store. (Candle shops work too.) Ravenous Beasts are known to suffer from sensitive snouts and severe allergies. Any strong scent will overwhelm them, causing them enough distress for you to make your escape. (Note: Don't forget to choose a location with a back door.)

# THE EXTRATERRESTRIALS

An Extraterrestrial's physical appearance is almost always unusual by human standards. Their eyes are either too large or there are too many of them, and some ETs have tentacles where legs should be. These Nightmares come from places you've never seen or heard of—distant worlds where they practice weird rituals and eat bizarre things. For these reasons, it's perfectly understandable that an Extraterrestrial might make its way into your nightmares.

But before you do anything, it's important to figure out which kind of Extraterrestrial is visiting you. There are two basic types:

- **The Tourists** are here for a visit. Think of them as intergalactic vacationers. They're generally pleasant and respectful. (A few seem to think

Earth is a zoo, but these individuals are unlikely to get too close to you.) If you meet a Tourist in the Netherworld, you can turn your Nightmare from frightening to fun by greeting it with an open mind and a little hospitality. Who knows? You might even make a new friend. (And who doesn't want a friend with a spaceship?)

◆ **The Gourmets,** on the other hand, have flown across the galaxy to eat us. This chapter deals only with the Tourists. Please consult the Gobblers chapter for instructions on dealing with the Gourmets.

## FUN FACT!

Extraterrestrials are very curious about our species. Sometimes their curiosity can get annoying. If you are beamed aboard an alien ship and it looks as if the creatures there would like to examine you, just say no thank you. Galactic treaties forbid the examination of any intelligent species without its consent. Domesticated animals are off-limits as well.

# PRO TIP!

Has it ever occurred to you that you might seem just as strange to Extraterrestrials as they seem to you? Perhaps on the planet they come from, only criminals wear shoes and cheese is considered pet food.

It's normal to be uncomfortable around beings you've just met. (Note: This also applies to new neighbors, classmates, and teachers.) But there's no reason to be scared. Instead of avoiding these newbies, try getting to know them. They're probably much less frightening than they seem.

# UFOS

Unidentified Flying Objects are popular in both the Netherworld and the Dream Realm. In other words, they aren't always scary. So the next time you're visited by a Nightmare UFO, try to turn the experience into one of your best dreams.

UFOs are "unidentified," which makes them mysterious. No one knows where they come from, how they work, or what kinds of creatures are behind the wheel. However, the qualities that make them mysterious also make them pretty darned interesting. If you are fortunate enough to have a close encounter with a UFO, you may get to do things that no human being has ever done before. Take advantage of the opportunity! You could be the first of our kind to greet visitors from another planet. Or you could be the first to test-drive the latest alien spaceship technology.

If you're really lucky, you may even get a quick tour of Pluto.

UFOs (like many other types of Nightmare) frighten some people because they seem new or different or weird. Take a moment and ask yourself: Do you want to be the kind of person who runs away from the mysterious? Or would you rather be the sort who runs *toward* it? There's no right answer, of course. But the Netherworld will be a lot less terrifying if you're able to embrace the mysterious instead of fearing it.

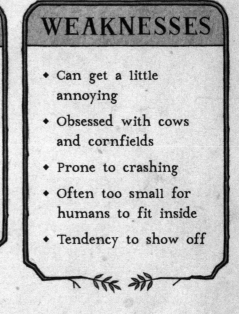

## STRENGTHS

- Incredible speed
- Advanced technology
- Tractor beams (We still haven't figured these out.)
- Pretty lights
- Difficult to photograph

## WEAKNESSES

- Can get a little annoying
- Obsessed with cows and cornfields
- Prone to crashing
- Often too small for humans to fit inside
- Tendency to show off

Some nights you're just not in the mood for visitors from another planet. If you're not feeling social, your alien friends will understand. Write a note asking for a rain check and leave it pinned to the roof of your Netherworld house or (for safety reasons) taped to an upstairs window.

## Poppy and the Alien

The timing couldn't have been any worse. Two weeks before she was due to have a baby, Poppy's mother was abducted by Netherworld aliens. Poppy heard the spacecraft arrive one evening after she and her family had gone to sleep. It hovered over her Netherworld house for a minute or two—just long enough for Poppy to bolt outside for a better look. As soon as she reached the front yard, a bright beam of light shot out from the bottom of the ship. Poppy watched helplessly as her mother's sleeping body was sucked through an open window and lifted into the space-craft. Before the UFO darted off into the darkness, Poppy noticed a small creature standing in one of the vessel's portholes. It stared at her with giant eyes . . . and then it stuck out its tongue at her.

The next morning, Poppy woke up covered in sweat. At breakfast she said nothing to her parents, but she kept a careful eye on her mother, who seemed . . . perfectly fine. She was bright-eyed and bushy-tailed and showed no sign of having been kidnapped the previous evening. Poppy took a bite of her pancakes and began to relax. It had just been a nightmare, she realized, and that made her feel better.

Until she went to sleep that night and found herself right back in the Netherworld with a UFO hovering over her house.

Every night for two weeks, Poppy watched her mother be abducted by Extraterrestrials. Finally, on the fifteenth night, she worked up the nerve to do something about it. As soon as she reached the Netherworld, she packed two suitcases—one for her mom and one for herself. Then she hid under her parents' bed.

When the UFO beamed her mother up, Poppy went along for the ride, a suitcase in each hand. On board the ship, she expected to be surrounded by a crew of aliens, so she was surprised to be greeted by a single creature. He was small and rather helpless-looking, and he spoke in a strange, high-pitched voice.

The more time Poppy spent with the Nightmare, the cuter he seemed. Finally, she took pity on the creature and offered him a compromise. Instead of stealing her mother every night, why didn't he just come to live with their family?

In an instant, the nightmare ended. Poppy woke to find the sun shining through her window. When she went to her parents' room, they were gone. Her grandmother was downstairs making breakfast. A couple of days later, Poppy's parents brought her new baby brother home.

# THINGS WITH TOO MANY

There are few Nightmares more unsettling than Things with Too Many. (Although Things with Too Few are often just as terrifying.) Aside from the famed Little Gray Men, almost all Extraterrestrials fall into this category.

The most common species of Things with Too Many include those with too many:

- Eyes
- Legs
- Arms
- Mouths
- Spines
- Heads
- Teeth
- Tentacles

WANTED
Reborn

This is not a complete list, of course. The important thing to remember is that even though a creature may possess too many, it doesn't necessarily intend to use them against you.

When you come across a Thing with Too Many in the Netherworld, try not to panic. Instead of running away, take a few minutes to observe the creature in question. Does it seem dangerous? Does it seem hungry? Does it seem emotionally needy? If so, do your best to avoid it. Otherwise, go on up and say hi!

**FUN FACT #1!**

In case you're wondering, Things with Too Few are most likely to have fewer fingers, noses, heads, mouths, and eyes.

Things with Too Many aren't always from other planets. Many famous Nightmares with Too Many originated right here on planet Earth. These include sharks (too many teeth), millipedes (too many legs), and spiders (too many eyes *and* legs).

## PRO TIP!

You may think that Things with Too Many mouths, heads, or teeth are the Nightmares most likely to eat you. This is a common misconception! Gobblers come in all shapes and sizes. Some of them don't even have heads at all!

# THE
# MOVERS

Have you ever woken up in the morning to discover that you're not in the same place where you fell asleep? Or perhaps you find evidence that you were unusually *busy* during the night. You might not remember having a nightmare at all, but you *did*. You dreamed about the Movers.

There are thousands of Movers in the Netherworld, and though they all operate in the same way, no two are identical. Late at night, they whisper in your ear. "Get up," they'll tell you. "It's time." And whenever you get the order, you'll find you have no choice but to obey.

What you do after you get up depends on your Mover. Some will send you down to the fridge for a snack of pickles dipped in peanut butter. Others will encourage you to get out your plastic nunchakus and fight the forces of evil in your mom's closet. Or maybe they'll just have you take the dog for a walk—at three o'clock in the morning, during a snowstorm, while wearing your Captain America pajamas.

Your parents probably call it sleepwalking. But *walking* may be the least of it. There's no limit to what Movers can make you do. Fortunately, there are a few simple ways to keep them out of your head—and yourself out of trouble.

# PRO TIP!

## HOW TO STAY AHEAD OF THE MOVERS

- Go to bed when you're supposed to. (Yeah, it's boring, but it works.) And make sure your bladder is empty. (That should be a no-brainer.)

- Put a childproof knob on your bedroom door. Awake, you'll be able to open it with ease. Asleep, you could need *hours.*

- Make sure your room is clean so you don't get hurt when the Movers force you out of your bed. (We know we sound like your mom, but this one is important!)

- Wear your least comfortable shoes to bed. They won't bother you much while you're lying down, but the moment you stand, the discomfort will wake you right up! (Just make sure the shoes are clean.)

# Ollie Tobias and the Movers

Even if you've never read the Nightmares! books, you may have heard about Ollie Tobias. No? *Really?* Well, he's one of the most ingenious delinquents in the continental United States. (We've heard rumors that there are a couple in Hawaii who could give him a run for his money.) So as you can imagine, Ollie needs no help getting himself into trouble. He's been a legend since the age of five. But no one in Cypress Creek will ever forget the week in seventh grade when Ollie began having nightmares about the Movers.

The morning after the first nightmare, Ollie woke up on his neighbor's lawn. When he opened his eyes, he thought it had snowed. Then he remembered it was June and he knew he was in *serious* trouble. Somehow—in his sleep—he had stolen the toilet paper from all the houses on his street and used it to wrap his neighbor's trees and shrubs. Fortunately, she was a sweet old lady and didn't press charges. She just asked that he clean up the mess.

The very next morning, Ollie woke up under the giant spruce tree in front of the Cypress Creek library.

He could hardly bring himself to peer out from beneath the branches. When he did, he saw the most remarkable scene. Somehow, during the night, he had painted a mural on the front wall of the library. Now, Ollie is a gifted artist, and his paintings are usually lovely. Not this one. Ollie's latest work was a giant portrait of the town's mayor picking her nose. This time, he didn't get off so lightly. He was grounded by his mother for two months, sentenced to thirty hours of community service, and publicly scolded by the town's highest elected official. (The mayor herself!)

It only got worse from there. We'd tell you the story of the following five nights, but Ollie is saving it for his memoir (which is bound to be a bestseller). He has, however, given us permission to tell you how he brought his nightly crime sprees to an end, in the hopes of helping other unwitting delinquents.

After an entire week of nocturnal naughtiness, Ollie finally realized what was going on. He didn't remember visiting the Netherworld, but whatever was whispering in his ear each night was turning the Waking World into one big bad nightmare. He needed a way to keep his body in his bedroom until it was time to get up and get ready for school.

At first Ollie thought of tying himself to his bed, but that didn't seem safe. What if there was a fire and he couldn't break free? (That was smart thinking on Ollie's part. Fires were a regular occurrence in the Tobias home.) So he decided to set a simple trap for himself instead. Before he went to bed, he left the door to his room open a crack and placed a bucket of ice-cold water on top of it. If, in his sleep, he tried to open the door all the way, the bucket would fall and the water would drench him.

The first night he set his trap, everything went wrong. The bucket fell when his mother opened the door to check on him, and her screams shocked Ollie out of his slumber. But the following three nights, the bucket trick worked like a charm. The Movers would send Ollie out on some mischievous mission, but the water would wake him before he left his bedroom.

Finally, the Movers gave up, and Ollie got a good night's sleep. In fact, the next day, he felt so well-rested and energetic that he decided to build a working volcano in a Starbucks parking lot. We'd tell you more, but that's another story for Ollie's memoir.

# The Life Suckers

Some Nightmares steal as well as scare, and the Life Suckers are the ultimate thieves. But these guys don't want your money or your cell phone. They'd rather drain your blood, energy, and hope. The greediest of the Life Suckers would be more than happy to take your life. But they can't! Remember—no dreamer has ever died in the Netherworld.

The most famous species of Life Sucker is the Vampire. While they're often very attractive, it's important to remember that Vampires are rarely as romantic in the Netherworld as they are in books or on TV. Developing a crush on a Netherworld Vampire is *not* recommended.

Other species of Life Sucker may not appear to be Nightmares at all. These species disguise themselves as friends while they rob you of your will to live. Frenemies are dangerous but easily defeated. As with other Life Suckers, recognizing them can be the toughest part.

Every culture has its own unique Life Suckers. If you plan to travel to other lands, it's a good idea to go ahead and identify the species of Life Sucker you could encounter during your trip. In China, a Jiangshi might try to absorb your life force. In Puerto Rico, you could meet a Chupacabra (though they prefer goats to humans). And in parts of Chile, you'll want to be on the lookout for a blood-guzzling snake known as the Peuchen. A little research is all you need to be prepared for a foreign Nightmare.

# PRO TIP!

If you have a nightmare featuring a bloodsucking Life Sucker, look for something (or someone) in the Waking World that's slowly robbing you of your health, happiness, time, energy, faith, enthusiasm, moxie, will to live, chutzpah, and/or benevolent feelings toward mankind—and dispose of it immediately! (Note: If it's a human, just stay away from him or her.) Then go back to the Netherworld and confront your Nightmare. With your regained strength, you'll now find it's easy to kick some Life Sucker butt!

# VAMPIRES AND BLOODSUCKERS

Most modern-day readers would say they know a lot about Vampires. We thought we did too—until one of us became friends with one. (Story to follow!)

It's a fact that Vampires drink blood. But it's not the taste of blood that draws them to your neck. Drinking your blood is simply the most effective way of draining your life essence. And as soon as you're at your weakest, Vampires can bend you to their will. When you spend time with a Vampire, previously interesting people become dull in comparison. Even the most beguiling pop star will suddenly seem boring next to a Life Sucker. Victims usually call this love. Those of us who know better call it blood loss.

## STRENGTHS

- Usually exceptionally good-looking
- Always incredibly cool
- Great eye-contact
- Sometimes sparkle

## WEAKNESSES

- Extremely bad breath, which they often try to cover with mints or mouthwash
- Poor conversation skills

**FUN FACT!**

It's true that Vampires don't like garlic. It makes their foul-smelling breath a hundred times worse. A string of cloves won't prevent them from showing up in your slumbers. But if you rub a small amount of garlic juice on your neck before you fall asleep, the Vampires in the Netherworld will probably keep their distance.

## PRO TIP!

The stake-through-the-heart procedure is total nonsense. You can't kill a Vampire because Nightmares don't die!

## Charlotte and the Vampire

When Charlotte was young, she had the misfortune to hang out with a Vampire. Every night when she fell asleep, he would appear at her Netherworld door. The Vampire was handsome and charming and extremely polite. He reminded her of someone, though she couldn't place who. She'd invite him in, and they'd end up talking for hours. (Note: Just like in the Waking World, the Vampire needs an invitation to enter one's Netherworld home; he/she cannot enter without one.) Each night before he left, he'd ask Charlotte for one favor—a small glass of her blood.

Charlotte figured that they were friends, and she had enough blood to spare. But as the nights passed, she felt herself growing more and more tired. Each morning, she could barely find the energy to pull herself out of bed. She might have recovered during her hours in the Waking World if it hadn't been for Gerald.

Gerald was one of Charlotte's closest human friends. It was amazing that it took her so long to realize how much Gerald and the Vampire had in common. Gerald never asked Charlotte for blood, of course. But whenever she saw him, there was something he needed to borrow or a favor he needed done. Charlotte always gave in. After all, Gerald was her friend.

Between Gerald in the Waking World and the Vampire in the Netherworld, Charlotte was completely drained. Until one night, the Vampire arrived at Charlotte's door and she discovered the word that saved her: *no*. She didn't let him come in, and she didn't give him a drop of her blood. And when she woke up the next morning, she felt strong enough to keep saying it. *No. No. No.* Charlotte said it to

Gerald—and to everyone else who wanted too much from her. Because she'd learned an important lesson: a real friend will never ask for more than you can give.

Gerald moved to Toledo, and Charlotte hasn't seen a Vampire in the Netherworld since.

# CHUPACABRA

Okay, let's get this out of the way: *Chupacabra* means "goat sucker." Go ahead and laugh—and then feel sorry for the goats. No animal deserves to have its blood drained by a hopping, lizardlike creature with spikes running down its back.

Unless you're from a Spanish-speaking part of North or South America, you may not have heard of the Chupacabra. And if you haven't heard of it, you probably won't meet it in the Netherworld. But there are lots of little "suckers" on the loose in the Netherworld, and when you run into them, it usually means something is eating at you. Not the *bite* kind of eating—the *something is bothering you* kind of eating. It could be a subject at school. Or it could be the girl or boy next door. It could even be the plight of the passenger pigeon.

Figure out what's getting to you. Then figure out how to deal with it. And until you do, don't let your Netherworld goats roam around after dark.

# FRENEMIES

This species of Nightmare is one of the most unsavory. Frenemies are wolves in sheep's clothing. A Frenemy will pretend to be besties with you when in fact he or she is your sworn enemy. They usually seem perfectly nice at first, but as soon as they get close to you, they go to work. The Frenemy identifies your greatest weakness and knows exactly what to say or do to make you feel small or ridiculous or hideous or dumb. They might start with a "harmless" joke that hits a little too close to home. By the time they're finished with you, you'll be blubbering into your pillow at night.

Frenemies adore attention and feed on emotions. The more you suffer, the more satisfied they feel. If they aren't stopped, they can drain you of your will to live.

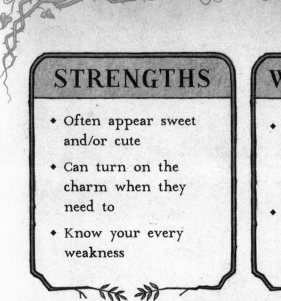

## STRENGTHS

- Often appear sweet and/or cute
- Can turn on the charm when they need to
- Know your every weakness

## WEAKNESSES

- Terribly insecure—usually about the same things they tease others about
- Need to be fed regularly or they will shrivel up and die

## FUN FACT!

Most people assume that Frenemies are always female. This is not true! Male Frenemies exist, and because they often go unrecognized, they can be far more dangerous than the females of the species.

# PRO TIP!

One sure way to defeat a Frenemy is to *starve* it. (Note: This works in both the Waking World and the Netherworld.) Do not give it the attention it craves. Either ignore it or walk away. If your Frenemy somehow manages to get your attention, do not allow it to feed. Whatever it says, don't get upset. The best thing to do is to say nothing at all. Just grin like you know what he or she is up to—and refuse to give it what it needs.

# CREEPY-CRAWLIES

Nightmares come in all shapes and sizes, and sometimes the tiniest can be the most unsettling. Very few humans can resist shrieking when a Creepy-Crawly slithers up their pant leg or scuttles across their shoes. Rodents, snakes, bugs, and spiders all belong to the Creepy-Crawly family. But any Nightmare that's small and fast can qualify.

There are many excellent reasons to avoid Creepy-Crawlies in the Waking World. For starters, a lot of them bite. But keep in mind that everything's different in the Netherworld. The Creepy-Crawlies that infest the land of Nightmares can't actually do you any harm. So if you have a bad dream about snakes or scorpions, why not seize the opportunity to observe them up close and personal—without ending up in the hospital?

Once you're no longer grossed out by its multiple legs or tartar-covered fangs, you might even consider making your Creepy-Crawly a pet. This may sound a little far-fetched, but the Netherworld can get pretty lonely at times, and you might be surprised by what pleasant and cuddly company a large rat can be!

## Creepy-Crawlies That Make Excellent Pets

- Rats (smart)
- Cockroaches (good for racing)
- Beetles (loyal)

## Creepy-Crawlies to Avoid

- Mice (not very intelligent)
- Spiders (only out for themselves)
- Millipedes (way too creepy)

# Paige's Army

Paige Bretter used to be scared of two things—Creepy-Crawlies and the Dark. In her worst dreams, she found herself being tormented by both of these Nightmares at once, and it always played out the same way. First the lights would go out and pitch-black would move in, surrounding her. Then a swarm of small flying creatures would arrive, buzzing around her head, crawling up her nose, and scurrying across her arms and legs.

Paige wanted to run, but she couldn't see in the Dark. She'd try to swat the bugs away, but they always came back. She knew curling into a ball and crying wouldn't solve anything. These weren't regular bugs, after all—these were *Netherworld* bugs. Then one night the thought occurred to her: *What if there's a way to communicate with them?*

Paige held out her hand and waited for one of the bugs to land on her palm. "Hi there. I'm stuck in the dark," she said, careful to keep her voice friendly. "Do you think you can help?"

The question had barely left her lips when a tiny yellow light appeared in the middle of her palm. She'd assumed the bugs were flies or gnats, but they weren't. They were fireflies.

One tiny firefly can't beat the Dark, of course. But Paige knew there had to be thousands of them in the thick cloud all around her. "Thank you so much," she told the bug. "Can you ask your friends to help too?"

The firefly's bright yellow bottom flashed out a code that its friends understood. In an instant, the Dark was gone, and the Netherworld was lit with a lovely golden glow. The swarm of fireflies settled on Paige's pajamas and kept their bottoms lit until she made her way to safety.

Somehow a bunch of teeny tiny Creepy-Crawlies beat the oldest Nightmare of all.

These days, Paige is still scared of the Dark. (Who isn't?) But whenever she visits the Netherworld, she has an army of Creepy-Crawlies to light her way.

# THE HOUSE MONSTERS

This species of Nightmare will give you the willies—especially if you live in a house that has plenty of nooks and crannies where monsters can hide. But you don't need to inhabit a run-down mansion to come across a House Monster in the Netherworld. Even tiny New York City apartments are known to have at least one House Monster hiding in a closet or under the bed.

The trick to dealing with House Monsters is what we call the Nightly Check. Unfortunately, you'll have to do it by yourself. If your parents check for you, there's no guarantee that they'll spot the creature that's waiting patiently for the lights to switch off.

So go ahead, get it over with! (Bring a flashlight if you need to.) Once you know that your house is monster-free, a good night's sleep will be much easier to achieve.

## Nightly Checklist

- Under the bed (and other large furniture)
- In the closets
- Behind the shower curtain
- Under piles of dirty clothes
- In the laundry room (Be sure to check inside *and* behind the washer and the dryer.)

## Feel Free to Skip

- The cellar/basement
- The garage
- The attic

The monsters that live in these places won't bother you in your bedroom.

# THE BOOGEYMAN

We're pleased to inform you that the Boogeyman is not real. Parents invented him back in the olden days to keep their naughty kids in line. (Clean up that mess/stop picking your nose/don't explore that abandoned mine or the Boogeyman will get you!)

Was it cruel to threaten small children in this way? Sure. But it was also effective (which is why practically every country around the world has a Boogeyman of its own). These days, most moms and dads have stopped scaring their children into minding their manners. But we've included this chapter for any kids unlucky enough to have old-fashioned parents.

# PRO TIP!

If you're having Boogeyman nightmares, there are two simple ways to stop them:

- Behave. (Okay, that's probably never going to happen.)

- Look him straight in the eye and tell him you know he's not real. This will take some guts. (Every Boogeyman is different, though they're all hideously ugly.) But if you can work up the courage to say the words to his face, he'll vanish in a puff of smoke and trouble you no more.

# THE THING THAT LIVES UNDER YOUR BED

Most Netherworld beds have a Thing that lives under them. When the lights go out, these Things creep into the room. Some just want to watch you while you sleep. Others prefer to nibble on toes. As unpleasant as it may be to have your toes nibbled in the middle of the night, we assure you that almost all Bed Things are perfectly harmless. Over the years, we've come to think of our Bed Things as pets. In fact, in many ways, they're even better than pets. They can be just as cuddly as a dog or a cat, but they never need to be fed and there are no litter boxes to be cleaned.

However, we realize that most of you probably have no desire to nuzzle up to the Thing That Lives Under Your Bed. If you don't want company after dark, there are steps you can take to keep your Thing where it belongs. First, you must identify which kind of Thing you have. (We know of five kinds, but there may be more.) Then give it something special to keep it content during those long, lonely hours when you're fast asleep.

- ◆ **Watchers:** Tape a picture of yourself to the underside of your bed.

- ◆ **Nibblers:** Offer it an old pair of your shoes—the stinkier, the better.

- ◆ **Sniffers:** Leave some of your dirty laundry on the floor at night.

- ◆ **Scratchers (rare, but not unheard of):** Scratching posts are ideal, but an old piece of carpet should keep them busy too.

- ◆ **Blanket Yankers:** Give your Thing its own blanket. It gets cold down there!

# THE SNATCHERS

These are the Nightmares that swoop down from above. One minute you're hanging out in your Netherworld backyard, and the next you've been snatched up and lifted into the sky. Most of the time, there's no warning at all—and that's the whole point. Snatchers prey on our fear of the unexpected.

Where you end up after you've been captured depends on what exactly has snatched you. Giant birds will usually take you back to their nests. (We once knew a kid who spent three dreadful nights feeding raw meat to a nest full of enormous baby birds.) Pterodactyls and other flying dinosaurs have been known to toss dreamers about like rubber toys. (And yes, some will eat you, though technically those Nightmares are Gobblers, not Snatchers.) Of course, there are also the winged monsters from books and movies—creatures like gargoyles and griffins. To be perfectly honest, there's no telling what these guys will do with you. It almost always depends on their mood.

The best way to fight a Snatcher is not to fight it at all. After all, if you're worried about being caught off guard, the best solution is to expect the unexpected—and be prepared. As it happens, preventing Snatcher attacks is much easier than you might imagine.

# PRO TIP!

These creatures want to surprise you. They won't attack if they think you're watching. So let them believe you're on alert at all times. Just take a pair of old glasses or swim goggles and paint two big eyes on the lenses. Before you go to sleep, make sure they're positioned on the top of your head so it looks like the two eyes are staring up into the sky. When you reach the Netherworld, relax and go about your business. Any Snatcher spying on you from above will think you're on guard and keep its distance!

# Other Kinds of Snatchers

- Robots with Jet Packs
- Cranes
- Things in Trees
- Giant Bats (Vampire Bats are Life Suckers, not Snatchers)
- Mutant Flying Insects
- Houses with Chicken Legs

# THE GOBBLERS

*Ohm nom nom nom nom nom*. You know the sound. You know the feeling. It's hard to say which is worse: the razor-sharp teeth of piranhas or the gummy toothless slobber of an Auntie Nightmare soaking you with her yearly kiss-fest. Either way, these horrible Nightmares will invade your sleep and haunt your dreams with the dreadful *nom nom nom* of their chomping jaws.

As you probably know, being eaten (or even nibbled) by a Gobbler Nightmare is pretty awful. We'd advise you to avoid them, but we're afraid that's impossible. Gobblers are so common in the Netherworld that sometimes you just can't help bumping into them. And as with other types of Nightmares, there's no point in running. Try to run from a Gobbler and you may get eaten every night for weeks.

If you need to beat several types of Gobbler Nightmares (which may be the case if you find yourself in a Netherworld zoo or on a Netherworld safari), we recommend investing in a nice suit of chain mail (you know, like knights used to wear). Nightmares' teeth simply can't sink through it. However, we realize that even in the Netherworld, chain mail isn't as easy to find as it was a few hundred years ago.

Thankfully, there's an effective repellent for almost every type of Gobbler. Figure out what type will work on your Gobbler and rub a little on yourself before you go to sleep.

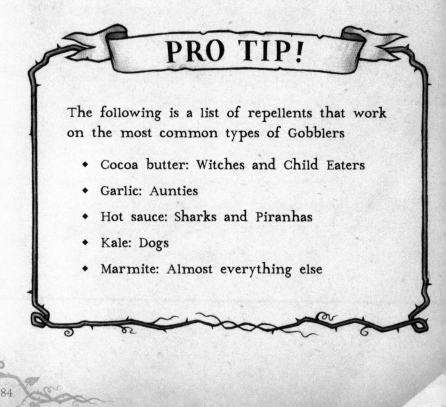

# PRO TIP!

The following is a list of repellents that work on the most common types of Gobblers

- Cocoa butter: Witches and Child Eaters
- Garlic: Aunties
- Hot sauce: Sharks and Piranhas
- Kale: Dogs
- Marmite: Almost everything else

# SHARKS AND PIRANHAS

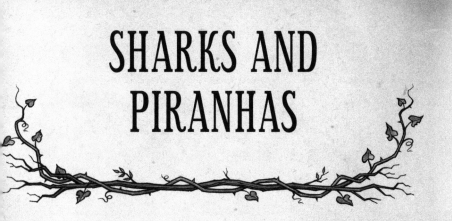

These two classic Nightmares have only one remedy: get in the water. Too many beach trips have been wasted by a fear of sharks. If you don't face your fear in real life, they will find you in your sleep—and your Nightmares are (most likely) the only place you will come face to face with an angry shark.

Get in that lake, ocean, or river. If your Nightmare swims are plagued by frantic schools of man-eating fish, then it's time to hop into some Waking World water and show yourself there's nothing to be afraid of. In the meantime, though, here's a side-by-side comparison of the pros and cons of getting gobbled by these water-dwelling Nightmares.

# SHARK VS. PIRANHA

## WHICH WOULD YOU CHOOSE?

**Shark:** One swift chomp
**Piranha:** A thousand tiny bites

**Shark:** Defeat one and you're done
**Piranha:** Defeat one and hundreds will still be after you

**Shark:** Would really rather eat a seal
**Piranha:** Would really rather eat something dead

**Shark:** Can bite a hole in your raft, kayak, or rowboat
**Piranha:** Might jump inside and take a bite out of *you*

# WITCHES AND OTHER KID GOBBLERS

At some point when you were very small, someone told you that you were so darn cute that they wanted to gobble you up. You probably thought they were joking. But the truth is, adults think children smell absolutely delicious. Fortunately, most manage to make do with a sniff or two. Some, however, can't resist a nibble.

So it's no wonder that fairy tales and nightmares are full of Kid Gobblers. They come in so many varieties that it would be impossible to list them all here. But there's one type that seems to pop up more often than others—and it's one we know well: Witches.

Fairy-tale Witches have been eating children for centuries. The Witch from "Hansel and Gretel" wants to roast them in an oven. The Slavic Witch Baba Yaga builds a fence with all the bones she gnaws. No matter where you travel, you'll hear similar stories (which—let's be honest—doesn't speak well for the weird adults who invented them).

If any of these creatures start showing up in your slumbers, you'll be happy to know that they're some of the easiest Nightmares to defeat. If you're very clever, you might find it fun to outsmart them. But in our experience, it's a whole lot easier to just make them barf.

## STRENGTHS

- Not very picky—will eat you baked, boiled, or raw
- Have a knack for showing up whenever you're lost
- Build their houses out of irresistible candy

## WEAKNESSES

- Can't stand the smell or taste of cocoa butter
- Prone to carsickness (which is why many fly brooms)
- Warty

No one's going to gobble you if they think you won't taste good. And there's one taste that's sure to make Nightmares nauseous. Believe it or not, Witches and Kid Gobblers can't stand the taste of cocoa butter. One little lick and they'll be too busy retching and washing their mouths out to go back for seconds. So rub some into your face, arms, and legs before you go to sleep at night, and you'll be able to dream in peace. You'll also wake up with beautifully moisturized skin.

**FUN FACT!**

In the Netherworld, Witch vomit has special powers. Scoop up a little and take it with you. No other Nightmares will come near you the entire night. You'll be able to explore the Netherworld all you like—or set off to rescue your friends from *their* Nightmares!

# DOGS: BIG, SMALL, AND DEVIL

Dogs may be man's best friends, but they're also the frequent stars of our nightmares. Every one of us will encounter a Nightmare Dog someday. It may be a Chihuahua that nips at your ankles, a mythical three-headed monster, or a gigantic hound with glowing red eyes. Whatever form your Nightmare Dog takes, one thing is certain: it wants to eat you. So don't try to pet it if you value your fingers. But don't run away either. Any Dog in the Netherworld can catch you in seconds. Instead, follow our simple advice, beat your Nightmare, and escape in one piece!

All dogs are omnivores—that means they'll eat just about anything. And humans are hardly the tastiest things on their menu. They'd much prefer a hot dog or a nice juicy steak. They'll only take a bite out of you if you make it easy. Netherworld Dogs are spoiled rotten and refuse to work too hard for their meals. So all you have to do is offer them something more delicious to chew on.

## STRENGTHS

- Big, sharp teeth
- Remarkably fast
- Slobber that burns through metal like acid (Gates can't protect you.)

## WEAKNESSES

- Bacon, sausage, all cured meats (Note: They hate kale.)
- Extremely lazy
- Can't stand the sound of Waking World dog whistles

## PRO TIP!

Bacon is extremely hard to come by in the Netherworld. (That's because it's the stuff of dreams, not nightmares.) But if you know a vegetarian, you may be able to find some in his or her nightmares. Don't worry about taking it. You'll be doing your friend a favor by removing the dreaded meat. With a slab or two in your pocket, Nightmare Dogs will lose their power to frighten. They'll be too busy begging for the ultimate treat to bother trying for a taste of you.

**FUN FACT!**

Slip a dog whistle under your pillow before you drift off to sleep. In the Waking World, these whistles will bring dogs running. In the Netherworld, they'll drive them away. So if your Nightmare Dog doesn't like bacon, just pull out your whistle and blow.

# THE AUNTIES

If she's supposed to be your aunt, why is she so much older than your parents? Why is she wearing so much perfume? Is a beehive still an acceptable hairstyle? Wait, she's *not* actually related to your mom or dad? Then who the heck is she? And why does her mouth seem to stretch so impossibly wide?

If you're in the Netherworld and you find yourself asking one or more of these questions . . . watch out! Chances are, you'll soon be hearing how much you've grown up. Or how cute you are. Or what a sweet little lady/gentleman you've become. And then, to your everlasting horror, you'll be gobbled alive.

Many children suffer from Auntie Nightmares toward the end of each calendar year. (Uncle Nightmares are less common but are growing more popular.) Thankfully, we've got some tips to help keep an Auntie from turning your Christmas Eve dream into a nightmare.

## STRENGTHS

- Perfume acts like tear gas, allowing them to creep in close.
- Special glands give them unlimited slobbering power.
- Surprisingly fast on the ground, with the agility of insects.

## WEAKNESSES

- Easily distracted by food
- If you can get one on her back, she can't turn over on her own.
- Encourage them to tell you about the good old days and they'll talk themselves to sleep.

## PRO TIP!

Gargle with garlic juice before bed. It's not only good protection from Vampires, it will also keep kissing Gobblers at bay. Unless, of course, your Nightmare Auntie is Italian.

# Jack and the Auntie

Jack thought he was dreaming about the most wonderful day of the year. He was still in his warm, cozy bed, and there was snow falling outside, just like in his favorite movie. He let out a yawn and stretched. As he drew in his breath, he was met by the smell of fresh pancakes and maple syrup wafting up from the kitchen. He was about to experience the best Christmas *ever*.

He quickly brushed his teeth so he could taste every delicious bite of pancake, then bounded down the stairs. He rounded the corner to take in the giant pile of presents he was sure Santa had left him. Then, strangely, the smell of pancakes began to give way to something . . . *different*.

His nose detected a sweet odor in the air—but it wasn't maple syrup. It was more like the sickly sweet smell of rotting meat. And as he inched closer to the living room, he heard the sound of an animal panting. It sounded like a very large dog.

Finally, Jack rounded the corner. There in the

living room were his stepmom, his father, his older brother—and the most horrible creature he'd ever seen. That was when Jack knew he wasn't in the Dream Realm. He'd taken a trip to the Netherworld instead.

For a fleeting moment, fear overtook him. The Nightmare was among the most hideous he'd ever seen. It had an enormous, tooth-filled mouth slathered in hot-pink lipstick, and it was surrounded by a cloud of stomach-turning perfume.

Jack tried to inch backward but felt his rump hit a wall that he was certain hadn't been there only moments earlier. The stench of the Nightmare was so strong now that his eyes began to water. But even though he could no longer see clearly, he could still make out the shape of her moving toward him.

"You're so cute, I could just . . ."

She didn't need to finish. Jack knew the rest. And suddenly his Nightmare-fighting instincts kicked in and he realized exactly what he was facing. He hadn't been expecting an Auntie Nightmare (though Christmas *was* just around the corner), so he hadn't prepared the usual way—by chewing a clove of garlic before bed.

Without any repellent, Jack had to improvise. She was coming closer and closer with every second. Any moment now, he was going to be gobbled.

Jack knew what he had to do. He gathered his courage and closed his eyes, then ran *toward* the Nightmare. He threw his arms around her in an enormous hug. "It's so good to see you!" he cried, and the second the words were out of his mouth, the dreaded Auntie Nightmare was *gone*.

# THE TORMENTORS

You've almost certainly met at least one Tormentor in your life. (If you haven't, you might just be the luckiest person on earth. Nice to meet you!) They can be bullies, vice principals, or librarians who seem to only know the word *shhhhhh*. What makes Nightmare Tormentors unusual is the fact that they often look a lot like the real human beings who've inspired them (except those in the Netherworld are usually bigger, hairier, or smellier than they are in the Waking World).

Of course everyone's (least) favorite Tormentor is the Clown. As creepy at birthday parties as they are in the Netherworld, these guys just won't quit! Some want to make you laugh; others want to make you cry. Either way, they won't give up until they have your undivided attention.

The good thing is, most Tormentors are more bark than bite. If you know how to deal with them, they'll usually go running back to where they came from. Once in a while they might even surprise you . . . and become *friends*.

On the following pages, we've provided handy tips for dealing with the three types of Tormentor you're definitely going to run into one night.

## FUN FACT!

Keep an eye out for some of the lesser-known Tormentors roaming the Netherworld. These include DMV employees, the makers of youth-size ties, tattletales, and that kid who always waits until you're looking before he eats his boogers.

# THE BULLIES

We just took a poll among ourselves, and we agreed that we would rather battle any Nightmare in the Netherworld (even a giant grub) than come face to face with a Bully. Bullies are the absolute worst. If you've ever been bullied, you already know this. If you *are* a bully, you should ground yourself immediately! (We trust our readers to follow the honor system.)

They may mock you and taunt you and give you wet willies, but the truth is, both Netherworld and Waking World Bullies are a rather sad lot. They only pick on people because they're horribly insecure. If only they could see themselves in action, they'd realize how awful they look and immediately mend their ways. (Okay, maybe not. Quite a few Bullies are just total jerks.)

You'll be glad to hear there are many ways to beat Bullies, whether you meet them during the school day or at night when you're fast sleep. We're going to give you just one—but we believe it's the best. (And those of you who spend your time inspiring other kids' nightmares, consider this your warning.)

## STRENGTHS

- Come in all shapes and sizes
- Know your insecurities (because they share the same ones)
- Feed off your sweat and tears

## WEAKNESSES

- Everyone hates a bully. Defeat one and you'll be a hero.
- Think they look cool but really look like total jerks

When your Nightmare Bully starts picking on you, surprise him and ask him to dance. We guarantee your Bully will be way too uncomfortable to bother you ever again. (Note: This may not work as well in the Waking World.)

## PRO TIP!

In order to battle your Bully, you're going to need a camera. An assistant would be great too, but if you can't arrange to meet up with one in the Netherworld, don't worry. You can take the Bully on all alone. All you have to do is secretly record him (or her) in action. The meaner he gets, the juicier your recording will be. When you're out of harm's way, simply upload your video to the Netherworld Internet and send links to everyone he or she knows. (Parents, teachers, and crushes are good places to start.)

# THE BOSSES

You may not have a boss yet, but unless you win the lottery or inherit a fortune from your great-aunt, you're likely to have one eventually. When you do, you'll probably discover that Waking World bosses can be awesome. But there are bad apples out there, and when bosses go bad, they can inspire some of the worst nightmares around.

Your Netherworld Boss might make you serve ice cream nonstop for hours, yelling at you the whole time for not making perfectly round scoops. Or perhaps she'll force you to clean Porta-Potties with a toothbrush or cook countless batches of cricket stew and taste-test every one. Unfortunately, these aren't just silly examples. We're sorry to report that there's no limit whatsoever to the torture a Nightmare Boss can inflict. That's why you need to put an end to the torment as quickly as possible.

## STRENGTHS

- Can never, ever be satisfied
- Can yell loudly enough to burst eardrums
- Are extremely creative when it comes to inventing new forms of torture

## WEAKNESSES

- Fine fragrances
- Are terrified of their own Bosses

## PRO TIP!

If you find yourself faced with a Nightmare Boss, the solution is astoundingly simple: get some lavender spray and apply it to your pillow. Not just the top—you must spray the underside of the pillow as well. How does it work? Well, Bosses think *everything stinks*, so when they encounter something that smells nice, they go running back to their Nightmare offices. You won't see them again for several days. (Bonus: the relaxing fragrance of lavender will ensure that you get a great night's sleep.)

Nightmare Bosses are very particular about their toilet paper. If you want to drive one completely insane, all you have to do is hang the roll so the paper comes from underneath rather than over the top. Just make sure you don't get caught. Your eardrums will thank you.

# THE CLOWNS

There are a million different kinds of Clowns in the Netherworld. Boy Clowns, Girl Clowns, Sad Clowns, Happy Clowns, Toy Clowns, Stuffed-Animal Clowns, even Regular-Animal Clowns. Over the years, we've learned a lot about these loud-laughing, rubber-chicken-carrying, big-shoe-wearing, red-nose-squeaking, tiny-car-driving fear makers. And we know exactly how to beat them!

## STRENGTHS

- Their high-pitched laugh contains a strong nerve agent that can render you unable to run.
- If they eat too many beans, they produce incapacitating laughing gas.
- They can fit an unlimited number of Nightmare companions in their tiny cars, making an ambush extremely easy.

## WEAKNESSES

- They can't stand being upstaged.
- Stripped of their makeup, they are powerless.
- If you don't pay attention to them, they'll forget you're there and wander off to bother someone else.

## PRO TIP #1!

Never accept a balloon from a Clown—especially the animal balloons. Trust us on this one.

# PRO TIP #2!

Defeating a Nightmare Clown is actually much simpler than you might think. Just learn three great jokes. These can be borrowed from joke books, parents, or friends at school. Surprisingly, "parent jokes" work especially well against Clowns. Jokes parents tell are usually more confusing and eye-rolly than they are funny. They'll leave most Nightmare Clowns scratching their heads long enough for you to simply walk away.

## Veronica and the Creepy Clown

When Veronica and Charlotte were young, they discovered a portal to the Netherworld and set off on a quest. Their hope was to bring an end to the terrifying Nightmares that filled their slumbers and left them exhausted day after day.

Charlotte's Nightmare was a snake-haired Gorgon

named Basil Meduso. Veronica's was a terrifying Clown who tormented her night after night with terrible jokes, endless gags (beware the whoopee cushion), and a high-pitched cackle that revealed a mouthful of razor-sharp yellow teeth. As you can imagine, Veronica was desperate to be free from this nocturnal carnival of horror.

One day in the Waking World, Veronica invited Charlotte to a sleepover, and that evening they ate dinner with Veronica's mom and dad. Now, Veronica's dad was the nicest man you could hope to meet, but boy, did he have an *awful* sense of humor. What made it even worse was that he seemed to think he was the funniest man alive. That meant Veronica and Charlotte spent the entire dinner listening to terrible jokes as Veronica cringed with embarrassment.

Charlotte didn't want to be rude, but she also hated to see Veronica shrink in her chair. Then she had an idea. She asked permission to tell a joke—and she told the only funny one she knew. Wouldn't you know it—the whole table laughed, *especially* Veronica's dad! Then he said something the girls never expected.

"Well, I guess I'm not the only comedian at the table. Looks like I could learn a thing or two from you!"

Veronica and Charlotte locked eyes. They suddenly knew exactly how to put an end to Veronica's Nightmare.

That very night, Veronica found herself facing the Clown in the Netherworld. At first she stood powerless as he told dozens of corny jokes—all through his jagged smile.

Finally, Veronica found the courage to put her plan into action. She shouted, "What do you call a fish with no eyes?"

The Clown stopped and stared at her. "Huh?" he replied, sounding completely confused.

"You heard me!" Veronica shouted again. "What do you call a fish with no eyes?"

"Well . . . I guess I don't know. What?" he asked.

"FFFSHHHH," said Veronica.

There was a long, painful pause. And then the Clown began to laugh. But this time it wasn't a scary cackle. It was a genuine giggle that turned into a guffaw and ended in a fit of hysterical laughter. Soon the Clown dropped to the ground, where it rolled around, completely powerless.

When the fit finally ended, the Clown looked up at the young girl. There were tears of joy in his eyes. "That's hilarious."

"Thanks!" she said. "What's your name?"

"Dabney," he told her. And this time when he smiled, his teeth didn't seem all that scary. (But they still looked like they could use a good brushing.)

# THE SPANISH INQUISITION

This is a Nightmare very few of you are likely to have, but it was once one of the more popular Nightmares in Europe. It made a brief resurgence when a British comedy troupe reminded us all of the most terrifying aspect of this Nightmare: nobody expects the Spanish Inquisition.

## PRO TIP!

History class is going to give you all sorts of nightmares, but should you encounter this very old Nightmare, the best solution is to try a very old trick: imagine your persecutors in their underwear. You see, very old underwear is very hilarious indeed. It will be impossible to be scared when you see that these guys' underwear was more complicated than a modern-day tuxedo. No wonder they were such nasty characters. They must have been burning up in there.

# WHAT TO DO

## YOU'RE BEING TORMENTED

We all find ourselves being tormented at one time or another. And we're all tormented by different things. Maybe your Nightmare is a Boss or a Bully. But it could just as easily be a Stepmonster, or a Saxophone Tutor. Tormentors can assume almost any form, but they all work the same way—pushing you to the point where YOU JUST CAN'T TAKE IT ANYMORE! But whatever you do, don't snap. Tormentors love it when they push you over the edge. Refusing to give them the satisfaction is the first step on the path to victory.

What to do when you're being tormented:

+ **Don't Feed Your Nightmares.** Tormentor
  Nightmares feed on misery. So even if you're
  upset, don't let them see it. Practice your poker
  face in the mirror before you go to sleep at night.
  If they can't make you cry, frown, or grimace,
  tormenting you won't be much fun.

- **Spread Good Vibes.** Sometimes when we're under a lot of pressure, we lash out at people around us. This just makes our own Nightmares stronger! So try doing the opposite instead. Whenever you're feeling low, do more good deeds. Say more nice things and tell more jokes. Even if your Nightmares don't go away, you'll be more popular than ever in the Waking World.

- **Bring Backup.** Everything's easier to deal with if someone's got your back. See if you can get a friend or family member to show up in your Nightmare. The Netherworld will feel a lot less frightening—and you'll have someone around to laugh at all your jokes.

# THE SIBLINGS

These are some of the most dangerous Nightmares of all. They look, sound, and smell just like someone who lives in your house. Sibling Nightmares can be so convincing that you may not realize you're in the Netherworld. And just when you've let your guard down—that's when the Siblings will pounce.

Sibling Nightmares know not only your worst fears, but also your weaknesses, and they have up-to-date lists of all your crushes. Some Sibling Nightmares are big and brutish; others are small and tricky. What they have in common is that they're thoroughly unpleasant—and in possession of information you'd rather no one else know.

Siblings will torture, tease, and taunt you all night. And unlike most other Nightmares, Siblings have the power to ruin your day as well. It's not uncommon to wake up in the morning feeling angry. When you see your Waking World sibling, you might mistake him or her for your Nightmare. At this point, squabbles may start. Insults may be hurled. Feelings will definitely be hurt. When the whole family is shouting and your pets have gone into hiding, you know the Nightmare has won.

# PRO TIP!

Fortunately, there's an easy way to beat a Sibling Nightmare. Unfortunately, you're not going to like it! You're going to need the help of your Waking World sibling. They're the only one who will know how to defeat their Nightmare double. Don't be afraid. Tell them exactly what's going on and ask for their help. You must join forces to defeat this Nightmare!

You're not alone! Many famous people have been tormented by Sibling Nightmares:

- Dolly Parton
- Julius Caesar
- The Pope
- Jason Segel
- Bruce Lee

# The Battle of Bernie and Elmer

Those of you who have read *Nightmares!* know that Jack Laird was briefly tormented by a Sibling Nightmare. But the Laird brothers were not the first residents of the purple mansion to find themselves in such a predicament.

When Charlotte Laird's grandmother was a little girl, she had two cousins who lived in the mansion. Elmer and Bernie DeChant were identical twins. And as twins, they were expected to share everything—including a room. For the first eleven years of their lives, the arrangement worked out pretty well. Until Bernie began having nightmares about Elmer.

In Bernie's Netherworld visits, Elmer was a mischievous imp who kept his pockets filled with Creepy-Crawlies, which he'd leave in strange places for his brother to find. Millipedes went in Bernie's shoes. Stinkbugs were tucked under the bedsheets. Once Nightmare Elmer even left a scorpion in the shower.

Every morning, Bernie would wake up from his nightmares with a thirst for revenge. He'd look over at his brother, asleep on the other side of the room, and he'd start making terrible plans. Then, at breakfast, he'd switch the sugar for salt. On the way to school, he'd push Elmer into a patch of poison ivy.

Of course, Elmer had no idea why his brother was suddenly so keen to torture him. Soon the two brothers were engaged in an all-out war. Wedgies were given. Heads were shaved. And many of the brothers' most beloved toys were put in the oven and burned to a crisp.

Finally, the boys' mother called a family conference and demanded to know how the war had started. So Bernie described the horrible things Elmer had been doing to him in the Netherworld.

"What are you talking about? That wasn't me!" Elmer insisted.

That was all it took for Bernie to realize that his Waking World brother had been framed by a Nightmare. That night the brothers banded together to catch Nightmare Elmer. They ambushed him in the Netherworld and forced him to eat all the Creepy-Crawlies in his pockets.

The next day, Bernie moved into his own room. And he never had a nightmare about his brother again.

# THE GIANTS

Giants are classic Nightmares. They were terrifying the masses long before anyone ever dreamed about UFOs or the Loch Ness Monster. Centuries ago, Giants were some of the scariest creatures imaginable (which is why fairy tales are so full of them). There are still a couple left in the Netherworld, but thanks to the Brothers Grimm, most kids already know how to defeat them. (Hint: Always chop down any beanstalks you find.)

The Giants that terrify us today generally come in either hairy or scaly varieties. They tend to be land-dwelling creatures, despite the fact that they are sometimes spotted emerging from the sea. (Large ocean-dwelling Nightmares are usually Lurkers, Stalkers, or Gobblers.)

Though they have been known to eat a sleeper or two, the fear Giants instill is that of being *squished*. Some wrap their arms around you and squeeze until you feel like you're about to burst. Others use their enormous feet to stomp their victims. A few will sit on you if they get the chance (which must be a very unpleasant experience, as Giants are not known for their personal hygiene).

When it comes to fighting Giants, there's one simple thing you must keep in mind: there is no Nightmare so big that it cannot be defeated. Every monster, no matter how enormous, has a weakness. Finding your Nightmare's hidden flaw may be tricky, but as soon as you identify it, even the biggest, hairiest, smelliest Giant will be at your mercy.

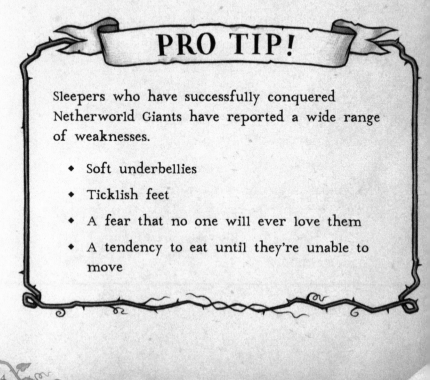

# PRO TIP!

Sleepers who have successfully conquered Netherworld Giants have reported a wide range of weaknesses.

- Soft underbellies
- Ticklish feet
- A fear that no one will ever love them
- A tendency to eat until they're unable to move

# BIGFOOT

Bigfoot (aka Sasquatch) and his cousins the Yeti (aka the Abominable Snowman) and the Orang Pendek have been popular Netherworld Nightmares for centuries. Large and hairy, these creatures live in the wilderness and enjoy terrifying visitors who accidentally wander into their territory.

As scary as they are, Bigfoot and his cousins are rarely dangerous. But if you come face to face with a giant fur-covered beast on a remote mountaintop, there is one thing you must never do: never, ever call them monkeys. Believe it or not, these creatures are humankind's closest living relatives, and most speak our languages fluently. Mind your manners and you'll probably escape with little more than a hug (see the next page). However, if you hurt their feelings, the punishment may be severe. On rare occasions, such creatures have been known to kidnap humans and put them to work picking the lice and brambles out of their fur.

## STRENGTHS

- Highly intelligent
- Extremely territorial
- Remarkably fast and agile
- Multilingual

## WEAKNESSES

- Nauseating smell that tells you they're nearby
- Very sensitive and easily offended

**FUN FACT!**

Bigfoot and his cousins are known for wrapping their arms around humans and squeezing tightly. As horrifying as this may sound, it's their version of a hug. You may not be able to breathe for a few seconds, but given the Nightmares' body odor, you probably won't want to anyway. So hold your breath and wait. They will almost always let go before you lose consciousness.

# GIANT SCALY THINGS: DINOSAURS, DRAGONS, AND GODZILLA

Every year it seems a different type of Giant Scaly Thing is in fashion in the Netherworld. Dinosaurs were big for a while, but these days Dragons seem to be all the rage. You'll still see a Godzilla now and then (usually when it's nighttime in Japan), but they're not as common as they were a few decades ago.

It makes no difference whether you're facing a brontosaurus or Barney. Every Giant Scaly Thing has a vulnerable spot somewhere on its body. Find it, and you'll be able to fight the beast and win. While you're trying to figure out where to hit it, there's one place you can usually hide in safety: underground. (Remember, these are Giant Scaly Things we're talking about. Smaller Scaly Things, such as velociraptors, almost always belong to the Gobblers species of Nightmare.) No skyscraper or fortress is safe from a Giant Scaly Thing, but there's no way a T. Rex or a Dragon is squeezing itself into a cellar or a subway station. So relax, take your time, and stay belowground until you're ready to kick some scaly butt.

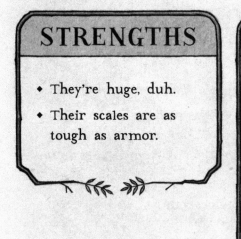

## STRENGTHS

- They're huge, duh.
- Their scales are as tough as armor.

## WEAKNESSES

- Most (with the exception of Dragons) aren't very bright.
- They can't squish you (or burn you to a crisp) when you're underground.
- There's always a small scale-free patch somewhere on their bodies.
- Dragons can't resist gold or a good taco.

# PRO TIP!

Giant Scaly Things are usually solitary creatures.
In other words, they don't tend to like each
other very much. So if you can find another
human who's being tortured by Giant Scaly
Thing Nightmares, make plans to meet up in
the Netherworld. There's a very good chance that
your Nightmares will forget all about you and
go after each other instead. And if you ever get
the opportunity to watch Godzilla fight a Dragon,
you should definitely seize it. (Just make sure you
stand at a safe distance.)

# THINGS THAT HAVE NO BUSINESS BEING BIG

If you've ever done any gardening, the odds are good that you've come across a grub. They're disgusting little creatures for sure, yet you probably didn't run away screaming. After all, most grubs aren't more than an inch or two long. But imagine coming face to "face" with a six-foot-tall version of the same nasty beast. Pretty revolting, right? Now imagine it can *talk*.

Icky little things often grow big in the Netherworld. Enormous spiders, earwigs, and cockroaches are far more common than any of us would like them to be. And let's be honest— even a kitten can be frightening if it's the size of a minivan.

If you encounter a Thing

That Has No Business Being Big in the Netherworld, you must not waste any time. The longer they're allowed to star in your nightmares, the bigger they're going to grow.

# PRO TIP!

**DO YOUR HOMEWORK.** Before you go to sleep again, learn everything you can about the creature in question. What does it like to eat? What likes to eat *it*? Is it dangerous—or just disgusting?

**STUDY IT UP CLOSE.** Gather a few small Waking World specimens and observe them closely. It might make the bigger Nightmare version feel less scary—or give you a few ideas about how to destroy it.

**START SMALL.** Sometimes problems that seem humongous are easier to deal with if you address them one small step at a time. One option is to start out by offering your Nightmare a bit of its favorite food. Then try to strike up a conversation. Little by little, you'll get more comfortable in its presence. And the more comfortable you feel, the smaller your Nightmare is going to seem.

# TROLLS AND OGRES

Trolls and Ogres differ in many ways, but they do have a few things in common. They're both large, human-shaped creatures that aren't very picky about what they put in their mouths. They would have fit nicely into our chapter on Gobblers, but since they're best known for their size, we feel it's better to label them Giants instead.

Fortunately, both of these creatures have been around for so long that the best ways to beat them have been known for centuries. If you've done your homework and read all your fairy tales, you already know what to do. For those who are a bit behind in your studies, we're happy to provide the answers right here.

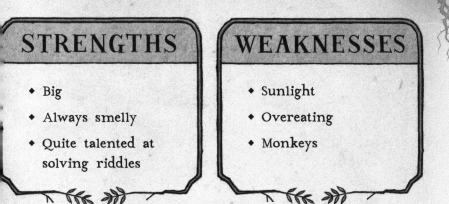

## STRENGTHS

- Big
- Always smelly
- Quite talented at solving riddles

## WEAKNESSES

- Sunlight
- Overeating
- Monkeys

## PRO TIP #1!

You may not believe this, but there were once Trolls roaming the Waking World. (There may even be one or two left in the coldest, darkest forests of Scandinavia.) Most are gone for good, however, because their kind suffers from a serious flaw: they turn to stone in the presence of sunlight. Now, sunlight can be hard to come by in the Netherworld, but even Nightmares need a dose of vitamin D every once in a while, so sun*lamps* are fairly easy to find. Get your hands on one and you'll soon be making lovely Troll statues wherever you go.

# PRO TIP #2!

Ogres also possess a fatal flaw, but theirs is a little more complicated. Once an Ogre starts eating, it will keep stuffing its face until all the food around it is gone. So the next time you find yourself hiding from an Ogre, gather as many rocks as you can and paint happy faces on them. When it finds them, the Ogre will think they're kids and shove them in its mouth like popcorn shrimp until its belly is filled. Not only will it be unable to move, it'll look so silly that you can't possibly stay scared of it.

## FUN FACT!

Oni are Japanese creatures that look and smell quite a bit like Ogres. They too will eat until they're unable to move, but there's an easier way to defeat them. No one knows why, but they despise monkeys. Just a single small statue of a monkey will keep them away.

# THE
# URINATORS

We've all encountered the Urinators—though most of us don't like to admit it. These evil Nightmares exist for one reason only: their goal is to make you wet the bed.

By now, you've probably learned how to defeat most Urinator Nightmares. However, there's absolutely no reason to be ashamed if one of them catches you by surprise. Urinators are some of the craftiest Nightmares in all of the Netherworld, and even experienced sleepers blessed with super-strong bladders are fooled every once in a while.

Urinators can assume countless shapes, either liquid or solid. In the land of Nightmares, toilets, swimming pools, and waterfalls are all likely to be undercover Urinators. In fact, if you come across a toilet in the Netherworld—and there's not a nasty creature crawling out of it—you've probably just spotted a Urinator in disguise.

There are many ways to conquer Urinator Nightmares. I'm sure you've come up with a few of your own. But there's one simple trick that will always help you stay perfectly dry until morning. Whenever you're sleeping and you feel the urge to empty your bladder, remind yourself of this fact:

*There's NEVER a good reason
to pee in the Netherworld.*

Do you clip your toenails in the Netherworld? *No.* Do you floss your teeth? *No.* Do you scrub behind your ears? *Of course not!* Nothing dull ever happens in the Netherworld—unless everything is about to go horribly wrong. So if you find yourself on the verge of doing something as boring as *peeing*, it means there's a Urinator after you. Zip up and wake up as soon as possible!

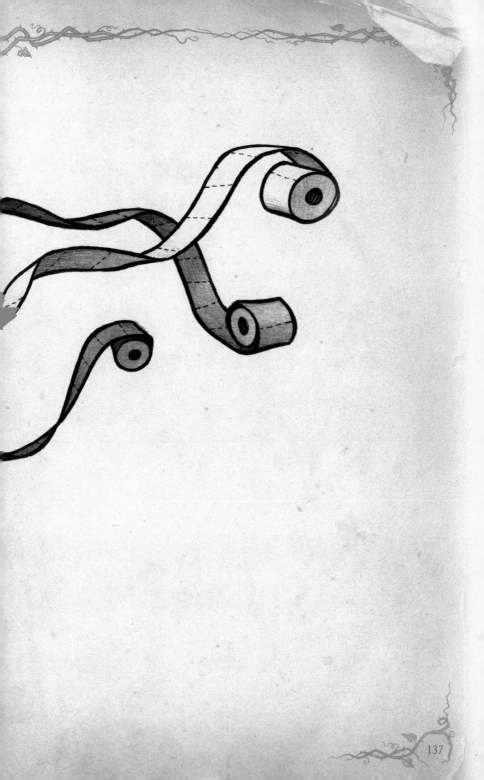

# THE LITTLE ONES

The Little Ones are particularly tricky Nightmares. They're small (of course) and often cute. But they're easily angered. All you have to do is steal their gold (Leprechauns) or be late with their bottles (Evil Babies) and they'll go out of their way to make your dreams miserable.

Wily and clever, the Little Ones can be hard to fight. So this is definitely a case in which an ounce of prevention is worth a pound of cure. When you're in the Netherworld, don't let yourself be dazzled by pretty wings, chubby cheeks, rainbows, gemstones, or buckets of gold. And as a young person, you should already know better than to assume that all small things are helpless. It's a well-known fact that a two-inch-tall fairy can kick a full-grown man's butt.

There's no need to run from the Little Ones (and no point either—they're faster than you, and a few can fly). In most cases, all you have to do is avoid temptation and walk away.

**FUN FACT!**

You may assume that Elves belong to the Little Ones family, but that's not the case. There are very few Elves in the Netherworld. If you've had a nightmare about a small creature with pointy ears, it was probably a Fairy or a Gremlin. In the Waking World, Elves live only in Iceland. Humans who have seen them describe Iceland's Elves as tall, regal, exceptionally good-looking, and well-groomed (particularly when you consider they live under rocks).

# EVIL BABIES AND CHANGELINGS

The people most likely to have nightmares that star Evil Babies are the parents and siblings of infants. (Sometimes visiting grandparents have Evil Baby nightmares as well, but they're able to put an end to the bad dreams by simply returning to their own homes.)

This is the point at which those of you without siblings pipe up, "Why would anyone *ever* be terrified of a sweet, pudgy little baby?" Those of you with younger siblings have already discovered the answer. Anyone who has ever lived in the same house with a baby will have suspected it of being thoroughly evil at one point or another.

Babies have been known to scream nonstop for hours. They will vomit peas, beets, and carrots on anyone who comes near them—and then expect you to clean up their poop. If that's not the stuff of nightmares, what is? How could it get any worse?

If you are the brother or sister of a potential Evil Baby, we have some tips that can help you. Sadly, if you are the parent of a diabolical infant, there's not much you can do. Don't give up hope. The torture will be over in about three years.

## STRENGTHS

- Their screams will drive you completely mad.
- They have perfect aim when they vomit.
- The smell of their poop can nauseate a whole neighborhood.

## WEAKNESSES

- They usually belong to someone else.
- They can't follow you home.

People used to believe that Fairies often stole human babies, leaving nasty little infant-shaped creatures called Changelings behind. This never happened in the Waking World, of course. (Waking World Fairies are far too smart to go around stealing annoying human babies.) But in the Netherworld, Changelings are everywhere. And if you're not related to them, they can be great fun to hang out with!

## PRO TIP!

There are three things you'll need to defeat an Evil Baby Nightmare: earplugs, nose plugs, and a rain poncho. Consider these your battle armor. While you're wearing these three items, there is absolutely nothing that an Evil Baby can do to you. Eventually it will get tired of barfing on you and crawl off to find its unfortunate parents.

# GOBLINS, IMPS, AND LEPRECHAUNS

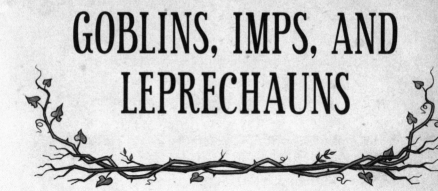

So you're in the Netherworld, minding your own business and waiting for your Nightmare to show up, when you see something shimmering beneath a shrub, inside a cave, or behind a sewer drain. You set out to investigate and discover a giant diamond or a chest filled with gold. *What should I do?* you wonder. Here's your answer: DO NOT TOUCH IT! Walk away. Quickly. And don't look back.

Few things sparkle or shimmer in the Netherworld. Anything that does is a trap. Put that diamond in your pocket or grab a bit of that gold and you're going to regret it. The Little Ones tend to rely on dirty tricks to get you. Touch their treasure and you'll find yourself enchanted, bewitched, or cursed. And things will go downhill from there.

As long as you don't get greedy, you'll be okay—though no one's perfect and mistakes will be made. If you find yourself at the mercy of Goblins, Imps, or Leprechauns, there is a way to break the spell.

## STRENGTHS

- Very clever and extremely tricky
- Once you're under their spell, they can make you their servant.

## WEAKNESSES

- Greedy
- Bad-tempered
- Always underestimate human children (who can be quite tricky too!)
- Never get tired of watching humans shine their shoes

## PRO TIP!

Greed will get you into trouble with these Little Ones. So it stands to reason that generosity will set you free. To put an end to your Nightmares, be as generous as you can during your waking hours. Donate your quarter collection to a worthy cause. Give your little brother the biggest slice of cake. Help someone who needs a hand. And then, when you go to sleep, find your Nightmare and face him. You'll probably discover you're no longer enchanted!

## FUN FACT!

Little Ones can be found in the Dream Realm too. Brownies, Gnomes, and Good Fairies make regular appearances in humans' most wonderful dreams. But always be sure to show them the utmost respect. Almost all Little Ones can cross back and forth between the Dream Realm and the Netherworld. (The exceptions are Gremlins, which are always bad.) Make a Dream Realm Gnome angry and he just might show up in your next terrible dream.

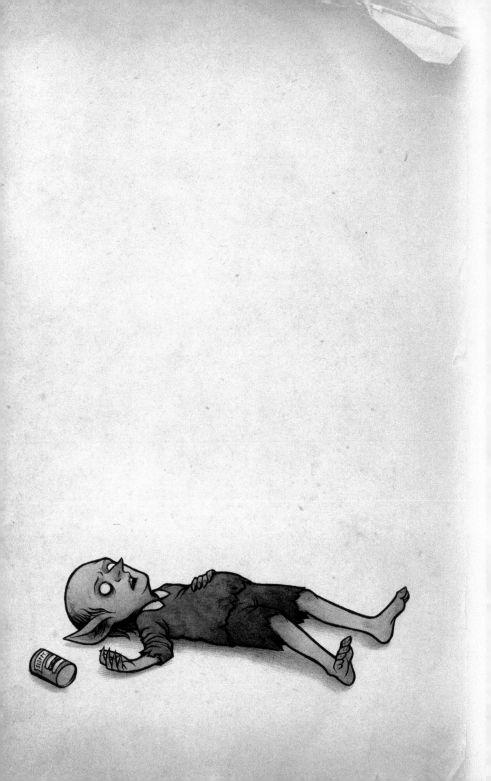

# THE TESTERS

You know what it's like. Everything depends on the test you're about to take. But when you look down at the paper in front of you, the words on the page turn to gibberish. Your palms start to sweat, and your heart is racing. If you don't ace this test, you'll never get into seventh grade and you'll probably end up living at home forever!

No? That's not what worries you? Then perhaps exams aren't your biggest concern. Maybe you're terrified of the Crowd instead. Night after night, you walk out onto a Netherworld stage. You see that the auditorium is completely packed. Then you suddenly realize you can't remember your lines. (And in the very worst nightmares, you're also totally nude!)

Or maybe you suffer from the worst Tester Nightmare of all—the one where a nurse is waiting impatiently in the hall and you can't relax enough to fill the tiny paper cup she's given you.

How do we know all about your bad dreams? Because we've had the same Nightmares—and we know just how awful they can be. So we're offering advice on how to beat the two most common Testers in the Netherworld.

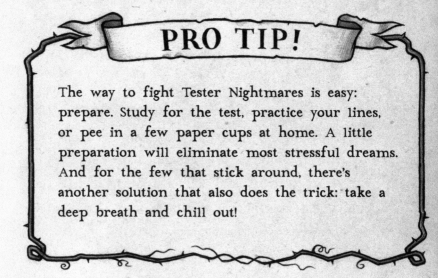

# PRO TIP!

The way to fight Tester Nightmares is easy: prepare. Study for the test, practice your lines, or pee in a few paper cups at home. A little preparation will eliminate most stressful dreams. And for the few that stick around, there's another solution that also does the trick: take a deep breath and chill out!

# THE TEACHERS

The Teacher is the most common of the Netherworld Testers. Even when you grow up, you may drift off and find yourself right back in your elementary school math class. These Testers are always trying to make you feel like you're about to make a total fool of yourself. Well, here's how to keep that Nightmare Teacher away.

## STRENGTHS

- Nightmare Teachers look exactly like your Waking World teachers, so it's hard to tell if you're dreaming.
- They know what you know, and they know what you don't know.
- They are especially powerful when you have a big day ahead.

## WEAKNESSES

- They can't scare you if you're prepared.
- They never change, so once you learn to recognize them, they lose their power.
- They are allergic to citrus.

## FUN FACT!

The Teachers we face in the Netherworld are imposters. Real teachers can only be found in the Dream Realm and the Waking World. If you're ever confused, there's an easy way to tell the difference: real teachers try to give you something, while Nightmare Teachers always try to take something away.

# PRO TIP!

Do the extra-credit problems in your math
homework. (Don't worry, that's not the whole
tip.) Then, about an hour before bed, eat one
extra-large piece of apple with a sprinkle
of brown sugar and a dash of lemon juice.
There is no scientific research to explain
why this works, but a math teacher who
dabbled in Netherworld alchemy developed
this recipe. According to her, teachers have
spread the myth for centuries that they like
apples specifically to trick their students out
of having them on hand for this remedy.
You can test this theory by bringing your
teachers an orange instead of an apple. See
how they react.

# Samantha Snaps

Samantha was late for her eighth-grade algebra test as she walked down the empty hallway of her Netherworld school. It was strangely quiet, and it seemed as though the overhead lights had been replaced with dull gray bulbs. Samantha sighed. She'd been having the same horrible nightmare for *months*.

It had started haunting her right after she'd reached an important conclusion. A very secret conclusion that only she knew about: *I am not good at math.* She hadn't said the words out loud, but she thought them every time she saw a new formula on the blackboard.

Samantha stopped at the door to her classroom. A pop quiz had already started. She entered the room as quietly and as apologetically as she could. In perfect unison, every student silently looked up from his or her test and directly at her. They held their stares for what felt like an eternity. The Nightmare Teacher took a loud bite of an apple and pointed at an empty desk, shaking her head in disapproval as Samantha sat down in her seat.

Then the Teacher rose from her desk, carrying a single sheet of paper. Her eyes looked almost black as she set the quiz down in front of Samantha. The Teacher glanced up at the clock, then back at Samantha, and hissed with a sickening smile, "Take all the time you need."

Samantha looked at the wall and . . . the clock's hands were spinning *backward*. She turned her attention to the test. It had only three questions, but they might as well have been written in ancient Greek.

Still, Samantha picked up her sharpened number two pencil and brought its point to the paper.

*Snap!*

The lead broke. Which was strange. She hadn't even pushed very hard. Luckily, there was another pencil at the top of her desk. She picked it up and brought it to the paper to write.

*Snap!*

Again, the lead broke. She looked around, confused. Then, one by one, students began taking their tests to the front of the room and setting them on the Teacher's desk, complete. As they filed back and took their seats, Samantha realized she was the only student left with an unfinished test on her desk.

The Nightmare Teacher made an announcement: "We will all stay here until Samantha has finished her test."

The class groaned in unison. Feeling the pressure, Samantha reached for yet another pencil.

*Snap!*

And another.

*Snap!*

And another.

*Snap!*

Samantha could feel the tension in the room. The students were getting angry. One after another, they began taunting and teasing her. Then came the pestering—begging her to finish the test. Samantha was helpless. She looked to the Teacher but found only the cold black eyes of her Nightmare.

"That's enough for now," the Teacher said. "See you again tomorrow night, Samantha." And then the Nightmare snapped her fingers.

Samantha popped up in her bed, drenched in sweat. But instead of being scared, she was *angry*. She was tired of suffering through the same Nightmare every night. She was sick of the Teacher, the pencils, and the quiz. It was time to end it once and for all.

She looked over at the clock on her bedside table. It was 5:43 a.m. Samantha smiled. There was plenty of time to get started. She pulled her math textbook out of her backpack and opened it to that week's lesson. No matter how long she had to study, Samantha was determined to ace the next test.

Guess what? She did! From that point on, Samantha wasn't scared of the Teacher—she knew how to defeat her. Do your homework, study for tests—and always keep a pencil sharpener beside you!

# THE CROWD

The Crowd isn't a single creature. It's made up of multiple faces. There might be five, or there might be five thousand. But their eyes are all glaring right at *you*—and you suddenly have no idea what you're supposed say. The Crowd has the power to scare most humans—even those who love to perform. As you might have guessed, shyer types find it particularly terrifying.

In the Netherworld, you're never really safe from the Crowd. It can show up in almost any setting, whether it's a classroom, a Costco, or a concert hall. Luckily, there's one less thing to worry about these days. In the twenty-first-century Netherworld, most Crowds don't carry torches and pitchforks. (Though we *have* seen a few throwbacks recently. Let's hope it's not the beginning of a trend!)

The Crowd will do its best to convince you that you're outnumbered and that resistance is futile—but take our word for it, this Nightmare can be defeated. In fact, there are two ways to do it. The first is uncomfortable but only needs to be done once. The second is easier but must be repeated every time you confront a new Nightmare.

## STRENGTHS

- It has you outnumbered.
- Its eyes can burn holes through you.
- Its gaze will give you a temporary case of amnesia.

## WEAKNESSES

- It looks hilarious in tutus, top hats, bike shorts, and hoop skirts.
- It is easily won over with slapstick.

## PRO TIP #1!

Volunteer to perform in your school talent show. You don't have to go it alone! Get your friends to join you in a skit or a song. You can even reenact a scene from your favorite movie. The whole point is to have fun. Once you've had a blast on stage, the Crowd won't have the power to frighten you anymore.

# PRO TIP #2!

We've all heard the most common advice for facing a crowd: imagine them in their underwear. Frankly, that sounds rather gross. There are a lot of people out there whose underwear needs to stay *under*. But if you find boxer shorts hilarious, by all means, go for it. That's the whole point! Whatever makes you chuckle will do the trick. We know a kid who likes to imagine his Crowd wearing spandex luge suits. (Just be careful. If you think of something too funny, you might pee your pants laughing.)

# THE NOT-SO-DEARLY DEPARTED

One of the first things everyone notices about the Netherworld is that there seem to be an awful lot of graveyards there. We assure you, this is not a coincidence. Burial places (cemeteries, crypts, catacombs, tombs, necropolises, and the Gowanus Canal) are the number one most popular setting for nightmares. (Number two is school. Number three is New York City—probably because it gets destroyed in half the action movies you see.)

Most living human beings are terrified of the dead. Which doesn't make much sense when you think about it. The dead were once people too! And some of them have fascinating stories to tell. Mummies tend to know a lot about ancient Egypt, and Skeletons are excellent history tutors. We recommend getting to know a few of each.

In this chapter we focus on three classic Not-So-Dearly-Departed Nightmares: Ghosts, Skeletons, and Mummies. (Vampires are covered in the Life Suckers chapter, and you can find tips for battling Zombies in our coverage of Chasers.) If you're having bad dreams about Ghosts, Skeletons, or Mummies, it's possible that you've been watching too many scary shows on TV. But in our experience, Nightmares of this sort usually mean that something from your past is haunting you.

## PRO TIP!

Want to stop meeting up with the Netherworld dead? Then figure out what's haunting you! There's probably something you haven't dealt with. Maybe you upset a friend a few days ago and still haven't apologized. Maybe you broke your dad's favorite casserole dish and haven't found the guts to come clean. Or perhaps you drew on the walls in your house and let your little brother take the blame. As soon as your conscience is clear, you can lay your fears to rest.

# GHOSTS

Do you have any idea how unbelievably boring it is to be a Ghost? It's one of the least popular jobs in the Netherworld. Gobblers get to eat. Snatchers get to snatch. But what do Ghosts get to do? Not a whole heck of a lot. Even the Japanese Yurei, the scariest Ghosts in the world (if you ask us), don't do much except crawl around creepily.

Now that you know the truth about Ghosts, what are you scared of? They're not going to *do* anything to you. And you've probably seen a million scarier things on TV. So why run away? Stay put and have a nice chat with your Ghost. It'll be so grateful for the company that it may even tell you exactly what you need to do in the Waking World to make it go away for good. (More often than not, you'll need to say you're sorry for something you've done.)

Poltergeists are the exception. These Ghosts don't just stand around trying to look scary. They're more than happy to throw things at you to get your attention. Be prepared to dodge some books, dishes, and small electronic devices before they're ready to talk!

Ghosts who take a liking to you become Friendly Ghosts. These are some of the best friends you can have, and their ability to go invisible makes them excellent spies.

# SKELETONS AND MUMMIES

If your Nightmares are Skeletons and Mummies, you should consider yourself very lucky indeed. We always know we're in for eight interesting hours when one of these creatures shows up in our bad dreams. Most Nightmares just disappear when you prove you're not frightened. Skeletons and Mummies, on the other hand, may be willing to show you the time of your life. Skeptical? Think about it. Mummies hail from ancient Egypt, which is one of the most fascinating places that ever existed. Make friends with a Mummy and you could end up touring the pyramids, exploring ancient tombs, or going on a cruise down the Nile River.

As for Skeletons, it's a little-known fact that most Netherworld Skeletons are actually retired pirates—and they know exactly where to find an adventure. You might sail to deserted tropical islands, fight crocodiles, or dig up buried treasure.

So don't hold the fact that Mummies and Skeletons are dead against them. Just make sure you're polite and prepared to follow instructions. Both of these Nightmares have been known to curse human beings they find lazy, obnoxious, or otherwise unpleasant.

## STRENGTHS

- Traditionally thought of as frightening
- Will curse you if you're rude, obnoxious, or boring

## WEAKNESSES

- Not really interested in scaring you
- Would rather hang out and swap stories
- Need to be careful with what's left of their bodies—they're not getting any younger!

# PRO TIP!

How do you show Skeletons or Mummies that you're not afraid of them? Not running away is a very good start. Stand your ground—then make use of our foolproof friend-making technique. Simply ask them about themselves. Where do they come from? What did they do while they were alive? How are they enjoying their new careers? Your questions will show the Nightmares that you're genuinely interested. And we promise the answers are going to be fascinating.

## FUN FACT!

Skeletons and Mummies know all the best spots in the Netherworld—and they've been around long enough to be VIPs. Get to know one well enough and he or she (sometimes it's impossible to tell) may take you behind the scenes.

# THE ALL MIXED~UP

Back in the ancient Waking World, humankind believed in some pretty freaky monsters. Quite a few of them were said to be half human and half beast. The following were (and continue to be) among the most famous:

- **Minotaur:** A creature with a bull's head and a man's body.

- **Gorgon:** A monster that resembles a human from the waist up, a serpent from the waist down, and has snakes for hair.

- **Mermaid or Merman:** A monster that is human from the waist up and fish from the waist down. Both females and males have beautiful singing voices. (You probably didn't know that they aren't very nice.)

- **Harpy:** A creature with a woman's head and a bird's body.

- **Centaur:** A creature that is human from the waist up, horse from the waist down.

Once, these monsters (and countless other half-and-halfers) spent their nights terrifying the people of the ancient world. Now they're not as in demand in the Netherworld. A few, like the Gorgon Medusa, will always be classics. (Come on, she turns people to *stone*! How awesome is that?) But most will only show up in your nightmares if you've been reading too much mythology.

## PRO TIP!

Mixed-Up Nightmares are very sensitive about the fact that they're no longer as frightening as they used to be. So show a little compassion the next time you meet one in the Netherworld. If you have the time, play along for a little while, just to let them think they've still got it.

**FUN FACT!** There's a support group for Mixed-Up Nightmares that meets every Tuesday at noon at the Netherworld courthouse. If your Nightmare seems upset that you're not screaming in terror, make sure they know they're not alone.

# THE SMOTHERERS

You'll know you're stuck with a Smotherer Nightmare when breathing becomes a chore. You just can't seem to suck enough air into your lungs. It might feel like something huge is sitting on your chest. Or perhaps you have the sensation of swimming in a pool filled with Jell-O. Either way, you're experiencing one of the Netherworld's most unpleasant dreams.

The first thing to do is *relax*. Easier said than done, we know, but the more you struggle, the more terrible your Nightmare will get. Keep in mind that no matter how awful the situation you're in, you're always perfectly safe. No harm will come to you in the Netherworld.

The second thing you must do is figure out exactly what's smothering you. There's usually something in the Waking World that's responsible. Is it a person who's always up in your business and refuses to give you space? (Relatives are a common inspiration for Smotherer Nightmares.) Or is it a situation that makes you feel stuck and helpless (like your meanest cousin's bat mitzvah)? Once you identify the source of your Nightmares, you'll be ready to take action.

## PRO TIP #1!

If your Smotherer Nightmare is inspired by a person in the Waking World, just tell that person you need some space. (Make sure you're polite, though, or this whole approach could backfire.) They'll probably give it to you. Even if they don't, you'll have found the guts to stand up for yourself. You may be annoyed, but you won't be afraid.

## PRO TIP #2!

If it's a situation that's smothering you, you must plan an escape route. That doesn't mean running away, of course! (Remember, you must never run away from a Nightmare.) Figure out exactly what to do to set yourself free. Make a list of all the small steps you'll have to take. Then start with the first step immediately. By step three, we promise you'll be feeling much better.

# BLOBS

Blobs don't seem all that scary at first. A giant glob of goo can be pretty disgusting, of course, but it's not the sort of thing that will make you run away screaming in terror. That's exactly how they trick you as they get closer and closer. Almost all Blobs go for the legs first. Little by little, you're surrounded. It's when you realize you're stuck that you start to freak out. And that, we're afraid, is the worst thing you can do.

One common type of Blob is Quicksand (which most people don't realize is a Blob at all). It's been featured in so many Nightmares, adventure books, and horror movies that many humans know how to escape from it. The same tips will work for any other kind of Blob (with the exception of Man-Eating Blobs, which are technically Gobblers).

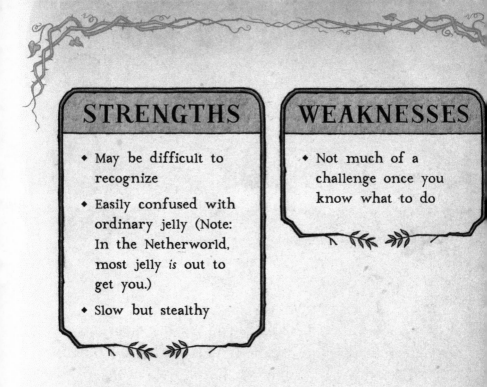

## STRENGTHS

- May be difficult to recognize
- Easily confused with ordinary jelly (Note: In the Netherworld, most jelly *is* out to get you.)
- Slow but stealthy

## WEAKNESSES

- Not much of a challenge once you know what to do

## Types of Blobs to Watch Out For

- Quicksand
- Slime (including Snot)
- Jell-O
- Rubber Cement
- Extraterrestrial
- Man-Eating
- Unidentifiable

# PRO TIP!

Need to escape from a Blob? Here are the steps you'll need to take:

- Relax. The more you struggle, the harder it will be to break free.

- Toss anything you're carrying (unless it's another dreamer you're trying to save).

- Lie back and float. (If your legs have begun to sink, this is the point where you can begin to slowly pull them free.)

- Once your whole body is floating, take a few minutes to think good thoughts. Puppies usually do the trick. (In the Netherworld, these pleasant thoughts will cause your Blob to begin to disintegrate.)

- As soon as you're as cool as a cucumber, figure out how to set yourself free.

# PEOPLE WHO LOVE JUST A LITTLE TOO MUCH

Love is like cake: The right amount is wonderful. Too much can be nauseating. But there are many people in the Waking World who somehow haven't learned this important lesson. They're the ones who love you just a little too much for comfort. Perhaps they follow you around day after day. Or maybe when they hug you, they squeeze you too tight. They text you nonstop or hang on your every word. It could be your mother, your best friend, or the creepy kid down the street. Whoever it is, their love has gotten overwhelming. No wonder they've started showing up in your nightmares!

Now, keep in mind, the Nightmare creatures these folks inspire may not look like the person you know. They could show up as a horrifyingly huge stuffed animal, an emotionally needy grizzly bear, or a giant diaper-clad toddler. (These are some of the most common Smotherers, but this is by no means a complete list.) If you come across one in the Netherworld, it probably means that someone in your Waking World life needs to give you more space.

## STRENGTHS

- So sweet they can make you physically ill
- Always there—they never seem to need to eat, sleep, or visit the john

## WEAKNESSES

- Easily distracted by photos (or even rough sketches) of your gorgeous face

## PRO TIP!

The first thing you need to do is break free from your Nightmare. It's a good thing Netherworld Smotherers are so easy to fool. Tell them you need to go to the bathroom (the only place you can escape from them). Give them a picture of yourself to gaze at while you're gone. Then slip away as quickly as possible. As soon as you wake up in the morning, find the person who loves you too much and have a chat with him or her. Be nice! But be firm. Tell them that you appreciate their love and affection (and you should!), but you need a little alone time once in a while. (And not just when you're taking a pee.)

# THE WEIRDLY FAMILIAR

Imagine this—you're strolling through the Netherworld one night, waiting for your Nightmare to arrive. You turn into a dark alley (because the Netherworld is *full* of dark alleys), and suddenly you see it. It's not a Lurker or a Gobbler or a Bloodsucker. No, it's *you*.

At least, it *looks* just like you. Technically, it's something called a Doppelganger—a creature that looks, sounds, and smells like you. (If you have an identical twin in the Waking World, you may be experiencing a Sibling nightmare.) When confronted by a Doppelganger, most people will be so freaked out that they'll bolt. Some sleepers never completely recover from the experience. It's a shame, really, because if you can muster the courage to say hello, your Doppelganger could have a lot to teach you.

Doppelgangers don't talk much—in fact, some people suspect they might not be able to talk at all. So don't get frustrated when yours won't chitchat. Just enjoy the silence as you walk alongside it. It'll be able to show you anything you need to know.

Your Doppelganger often knows things about you that you haven't figured out yet. It may know that you're really great at rock climbing—even if you've never left the ground in the Waking World. It might know who you're going to fall in love with next, or it could know that you're going to develop an allergy to spinach. Spend a night hanging out with your Doppelganger and you will almost always discover something interesting about yourself. When this happens, it becomes less frightening and its power begins to weaken.

# THE OLD ONES

Every year a bunch of flashy new Nightmares appear in the Netherworld and seize the spotlight. (Right now the Netherworld is seeing a boom in the Robot and Tiny Dog populations.) There are a few Nightmares, however, that have stood the test of time. They're ancient—perhaps even eternal. We call this group the Old Ones.

The Old Ones have haunted humankind since the world began. They don't try to grab headlines, and they don't feel the need to be on the cover of *Nightmares Monthly*. They just exist, quiet and terrifying, in the background of our nightmares. The fear they produce is far worse than a scream or a startle. It is a deep, dark, knowing kind of fear—one that can be very difficult to escape.

**FUN FACT!**

Not all ancient Nightmares become classics like the Old Ones. Many just stop being scary. For instance, Bath Nightmares were common for thousands of years. People would do just about anything to avoid having to scrub themselves clean. These days, however, Bath Nightmares are only popular with the preschool crowd.

Eclipses are another Nightmare that didn't stand the test of time. In ancient times, they inspired countless nightmares. Humans believed that only evil forces could make the sun disappear. Now that we know the truth, many people actually go out of their way to see them!

# THE DARK

The Dark needs no introduction. It is the oldest, most powerful Nightmare in the Netherworld. There may be a few people out there who aren't afraid of the Dark, but no one can claim that they *like* it.

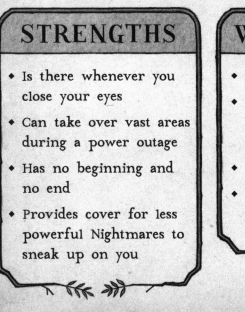

## STRENGTHS

- Is there whenever you close your eyes
- Can take over vast areas during a power outage
- Has no beginning and no end
- Provides cover for less powerful Nightmares to sneak up on you

## WEAKNESSES

- The sun
- Flashlights, overhead lights, table lamps, candles, and night-lights
- The moon and stars
- More than three people gathered together

# PRO TIP!

You can't run from the Dark. It will find you eventually, so you'd better learn how to face it. Fortunately, there's one way to conquer your fear: you must sit silently in utter blackness. This can be pretty scary if you're alone, so arrange a "conquer the Dark" sleepover with three trusted friends. After a nice dinner of hamburgers or pizza, prepare for the task at hand. With a flashlight by your side in case of emergency, turn off all the lights and electronics in your living room. Then sit without making a sound. Try not to breathe too loudly. Let the darkness overtake you. You'll feel safe with your friends beside you, so there's no need to cheat. Try to sit in the dark for five minutes without making a noise. If you can do it, then the Dark will no longer have power over you (at least for one night).

# The Emperor and the Dark

No one knows for sure if it's true, but there's a legend in the Netherworld about the power of the Dark. It's the story of a man named Napoleon, who was once the emperor of France and the most powerful person in the entire world (or so he liked to think).

Not long after his army conquered Egypt, Napoleon took a trip to visit the pyramids. When he arrived, he was offered a challenge that many had undertaken but none had completed. Napoleon was dared to spend one night alone in the darkness of a chamber so deep inside the Great Pyramid that light had never reached it.

If Napoleon was scared, he wasn't the kind of guy who'd admit it. He accepted without hesitation.

No one was with the emperor when he entered the chamber, so details are scarce, but soon after the door to the room was shut, something unexpected happened. The man who had conquered countless lands began to squeal in terror. He didn't last the night—he didn't even last an hour. (Heck, he didn't make it ten minutes!) Napoleon was heard screeching for help after a single minute. When his guides came to his rescue, they asked what had happened. Napoleon, white as a sheet, refused to answer. He commanded that the incident never be mentioned.

A few years later, when Napoleon was on his deathbed, one of his trusted advisors finally worked up the courage to ask the otherwise fearless leader what he'd seen inside the Great Pyramid. What could possibly have scared the emperor so badly? Napoleon looked up with a terrified expression and managed to let four words escape before he closed his eyes forever: "I saw *the Dark*."

# TIME AND THE GRIM REAPER

These two Nightmares have been best friends for as long as either of them can remember. Sure, they argue, but they always make up in the end. The Grim Reaper gets annoyed that Time always takes so long, but Time likes his hair to be perfect before he hits the town. Here are a couple of tips, should you encounter one or both of these ancient Nightmares.

## TIME

Time can't stand Hawaiian prints! It's the one fabric that renders him powerless. Get yourself some Hawaiian-print pajamas or pillowcases and be sure to get in bed up to twenty minutes before your actual bedtime. If it looks like you're relaxed and on vacation, then Time will go looking for a higher-stress dreamer.

## PRO TIP!

No one knows what Time really looks like. In fact, you might not realize that he (or she) is responsible for your bad dreams. If you're not sure, there are a few signs you can search for. Spot one of the following and you'll know it's time to whip out the Hawaiian print: ticking clocks, alarms, cuckoos, church bells, gray hair, the *Jeopardy!* theme, rushing rivers, dinosaurs, Betty White, hourglasses, rotting meat, unraveling sweaters, melting ice cream cones.

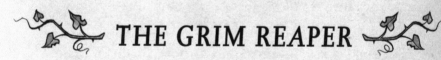

# THE GRIM REAPER

With his long black robe, razor-sharp scythe, and fleshless face, the Grim Reaper (aka Mr. Death) inspires terror in most sleepers. He doesn't even need to do much besides show up and look creepy. It's gotten that easy for him to make people scream. So he's not going to waste his nights trying to scare the heck out of someone who isn't afraid of him. Want to show him you're one of the few? Do twenty-five jumping jacks right before bed to let the Grim Reaper know you have no intention of hanging out with him anytime soon!

If you ever have the chance to meet
the Grim Reaper, be sure to check out
the outfit he's wearing under the robe.
It's a little-known fact that Mr. Death is
quite the clotheshorse, and his fashion sense is
renowned throughout the Netherworld. If you
can get him talking about his ensemble, he'll
probably forget to cut you down with his scythe.

# MOTHER NATURE

If you're wondering what's so scary about sweet Mother Nature, you've obviously never been struck by lightning or carried off by a tornado. Waking World storms can be terrifying—and the ones in the Netherworld are often much worse. But there's one big difference between the two types of foul weather. Nightmare Storms—no matter how bad—aren't able to hurt you. That doesn't mean they can't be unpleasant, of course. No one wants to spend eight hours being battered by baseball-size hail or getting swept away by typhoons.

When nasty weather hits, most dreamers assume there's not much they can do. We're here to tell you that's not the case. The trick to beating Mother Nature is information. Keep finding yourself trapped in a blizzard? Learn how to build a snow shelter. Worried about lightning? Find out where you'll be safest when it starts to strike. Not interested in a trip to Oz? Make sure you know where to hide out if a Netherworld tornado is coming your way. The more you know, the calmer you'll be. And staying calm can make all the difference.

This advice will serve you well even if it's not really a Storm that scares you. People often experience Storm Nightmares when the world around them feels like it's going a bit crazy. It happens to all of us at one time or another. The best thing to do is keep your cool, do some research—and start making plans.

## PRO TIP!

Pick your favorite flower and press it between these pages in the box below. Sometimes Mother Nature just needs a little reminder of her soft side. As long as the petals stay here, you should be safe from harsh Mother Nature nightmares.

# WHAT TO DO

## YOU'RE CAUGHT IN A NETHERWORLD TORNADO

You can see it on the horizon. It's heading straight toward you, ripping up trees and sending eighteen-wheelers spinning into air. It's totally terrifying, no doubt about it. It's also completely harmless. The worst thing a Netherworld Tornado can do is make you so dizzy that you barf in your bed (which *is* pretty gross, we'll admit). But if that's the worst it can do, why bother running? You can always change your sheets in the morning. So in this case, the "What to Do" is simple. Why not experience something that few Waking World beings have lived to tell about—being caught inside a tornado?

None of us has ever had the opportunity to experience a Netherworld Tornado, so we can't give you any advice aside from the piece that holds true for all Nightmares: if you find the guts to face it one night, it's sure to be gone the next. But we *do* have a few theories about what might happen once you're inside a powerful Storm. If you are ever lucky enough to have a chance to find out, please let us know!

# WHAT HAPPENS WHEN YOU GET CAUGHT IN A NETHERWORLD TORNADO (OUR THEORIES)

- You travel back in time. (We can't agree on how far back. Could be a couple of hours. Could be a few centuries. How you return to the present is anyone's guess.)

- You're taken to a distant land where witches melt and monkeys fly.

- You gain superhuman powers for a single night.

- You barf nonstop and never ride a Tilt-a-Whirl again.

# NOTHINGNESS

Nothingness is one of the most difficult Nightmares to identify. You can't see, touch, or smell it. Experts would say it's more of a feeling than anything else. It's empty, hollow, and absolutely terrifying.

## PRO TIP #1!

There is only one way to defeat Nothingness: fill it with Somethingness. It can be any kind of Somethingness you choose, but the easiest and fastest way to fill Nothingness is with music. Pick your favorite song and sing it before bed. Then, if Nothingness appears in your Nightmare, you'll be ready. Open your mouth and belt out a song!

This explains the creation of the lullaby.

## PRO TIP #2!

Think of Nothingness like an empty grocery bag. Before bed, use some of your happiest thoughts to fill the bag. Some examples:

- Amusement parks
- Cake
- Your parents
- Your grandparents
- Your friends
- A funny joke
- Your favorite movie
- Macaroni and cheese
- The beach
- Your birthday

The list can go on and on. By the time you're done, you'll realize there's way too much good stuff to be scared of Nothing!

# PURE EVIL

Until now, all the Nightmares we've profiled exist for a single reason: as scary as they may be, their job is to help you face your fears and grow stronger. But there are a few Nightmares in the Netherworld that don't have your best interests at heart. These are the creatures we call Pure Evil. Most existed before us and will continue to exist long after we're gone. We don't know what they want, and we don't want to find out. It's safe to say it's not good.

It's best to avoid the Pure Evil bunch. When you see them coming, head the other way. If they come after you, you'll need to stand your ground and fight. Rest assured, even Pure Evil has its weaknesses.

## STRENGTHS

- Bad to the bone
- Never play by the rules
- Have mastered the art of the evil cackle

## WEAKNESSES

- Terrible at making friends
- Breath that smells like rotten eggs
- Revolting table manners

## PRO TIP!

A good heart is the best defense against Pure Evil. But we recommend learning kung fu too. Know when it's time to stop being nice—and start kicking some serious butt.

# THE TALL MAN

Not everything Pure Evil is old. It was only a few years ago that the Tall Man began making appearances in the Netherworld. No one knows who he is or who first dreamed him up. We don't even know what he wants. All we know is that he's seriously scary. The chills he sends down dreamers' spines can be so intense that people have found themselves frozen in place.

**FUN FACT!** Learning how to recognize the Tall Man's distinctive scent will help you steer clear of him. He smells like burned marshmallows or the fake fog at a haunted house.

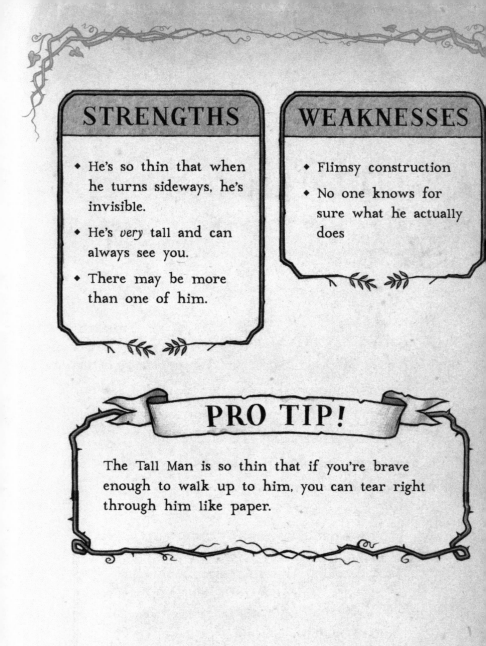

## STRENGTHS

- He's so thin that when he turns sideways, he's invisible.
- He's *very* tall and can always see you.
- There may be more than one of him.

## WEAKNESSES

- Flimsy construction
- No one knows for sure what he actually does

## PRO TIP!

The Tall Man is so thin that if you're brave enough to walk up to him, you can tear right through him like paper.

# Charlotte and the Tall Man

Charlotte first encountered the Tall Man face to face when she was thirteen years old. It's a good thing she wasn't alone that night. Dabney the Clown, her best friend's Nightmare, was with her. (If you're wondering how Charlotte became buddies with a Nightmare, please consult our Tormentors chapter.)

Charlotte had visited the Netherworld many times at that point, and she was pretty comfortable with how the rules worked. Every once in a while she'd have to face down a fear, but usually she visited the land of Nightmares to hang out with her friends. On the night in question, Charlotte and Dabney were on their way to their friend Basil's house. They were walking through a particularly dark stretch of woods when Charlotte thought she saw the shadow of a tree following them. It could only have been a tree, she thought, because the shadow was so incredibly long and thin.

Trees aren't supposed to follow you, of course. But strange things happen all the time in the Netherworld, and Charlotte wasn't all that concerned. So she returned her attention to the *very* long joke Dabney was telling (a joke he'd already told her on several occasions).

But then Charlotte saw it.

The long shadow moved again. And this time the Tall Man emerged from between the trees. He was *impossibly* tall and impossibly thin. And even though he didn't have a face, Charlotte knew he'd been watching her for years—not just in the Netherworld, but in her own world as well. Charlotte's heart dropped into her stomach, but she mustered the courage to ask the Tall Man what he wanted to teach her.

The Tall Man didn't reply.

Charlotte turned to Dabney and found that the Clown was far paler than his usual shade of white. He looked absolutely petrified, but he managed to chuckle a single word: *RUN*.

Charlotte was confused. The first rule of the Netherworld is never, ever, ever run from a Nightmare. But then she saw that Dabney was pointing in the direction that she needed to run. It wasn't *away* from the Tall Man. It was *through* him.

No one knows how Charlotte found the guts to follow Dabney's advice. But somehow she did. She took a deep breath, clenched her fists, and ran straight at the Tall Man. As she passed through the Nightmare, he appeared to come apart at the seams. You see, the Tall Man is so scary that most people never get close enough to realize that he's made of nothing but fear itself.

Charlotte won the battle with the Tall Man that night. But she's always suspected that he never truly went away. She hasn't seen him again, but she knows that doesn't mean the Tall Man hasn't seen *her*.

# DEMONS

No two Demons are the same, so it would be impossible to list them all here. Most of us have one, whether we know it or not. Demons are the wicked creatures who whisper in our ears and encourage us to do dumb, dangerous, or (occasionally) terrible things.

A quick fix for anyone having Demon Nightmares is to wear earplugs to bed. This will work for a few nights—until your Demons find a new way to communicate with you. (They're quite ingenious, actually. We know of one Demon who put up billboards when his victim kept sleeping with cotton in his ears.) But you'll be glad to know that there's a way to get rid of your Demons forever.

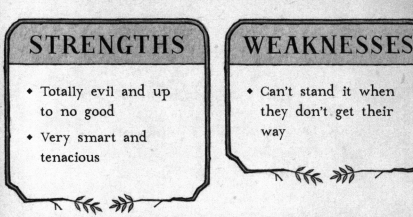

## STRENGTHS

- Totally evil and up to no good
- Very smart and tenacious

## WEAKNESSES

- Can't stand it when they don't get their way

# PRO TIP!

How do you send your Demons packing? *Listen to them.* That's right! Listen to your Demons—and then do the opposite of what they tell you to do. If yours tells you to steal, give something away instead. If it wants you to cheat on a test, study even harder. Eventually your Demon will get so angry and frustrated that it will explode in a ball of fire.

## FUN FACT #1!

Many types of Demons can't handle the cold. A bowl of ice on your bedside table, with a fan turned to medium behind it, will often repel these fire-and-brimstone-loving Nightmares. (Note: The fan must be on medium. High is too high, and low is too low.)

## FUN FACT #2!

(Note: HIGH-RISK) Kiss a Demon on its nose and it will instantly be rendered powerless. There is some evidence that it may also transform the Nightmare into your faithful pet for all eternity. As of this publication, no one we know has ever tried this.

# THE MANIACS

Maniacs are a truly terrifying breed of Nightmare for one very important reason: they are completely unpredictable and impossible to reason with. In other words, these Nightmares don't make any sense.

## STRENGTHS AND WEAKNESSES

Every Maniac has a unique list of strengths and weaknesses. If you're unlucky enough to experience one of these Nightmares, you must do the hard work of defeating him or her on your own. Sometimes it can take a while, but we promise you it can be done.

Below are the Maniacs we've come across in the Netherworld and their documented weakness.

## THE LIGHT STEALER

The Light Stealer is not afraid of anything. Except pigeons. Learn a pigeon call. Do it three times loudly before bed each night—or whenever you come across a Light Stealer in the Netherworld. This will keep it away.

## BRIAN

Brian looks like an ordinary guy, which is his greatest strength. He will haunt your sleep until you are so tired that you pass out in your breakfast cereal. To defeat him, place a small cracker with peanut butter inside a plastic baggie. Then slip it under your pillow. (Note: It is important to NOT include milk.) Anything you have under your pillow will appear in your Nightmare. With no liquid to wash it down, the peanut butter will glue Brian's mouth shut and distract him for hours.

# MEANIES

We saved this type of Nightmare for last because we know—for a fact—that everyone reading this has encountered or will encounter at least one in their lifetime. Meanies are exactly what you imagine they are—Nightmares whose sole purpose is to make you cry. (Or sulk—or at the very least whimper.) They usually look like people you know in real life—teachers or cousins or schoolmates. And inside your bad dreams, they know just what to say or do to hurt your feelings.

As we mentioned, all of us—every human being on earth—have Meanie Nightmares. Why did we stress that? Because if you can tuck that little piece of information away in your head, you'll have everything you need to beat them.

Allow us to explain. So there's someone who doesn't like you in your nightmares. Okay. Maybe they don't like you much in the Waking World either. Sound harsh? It's not. We all know people who don't like us. The reasons can be silly or stupid or just plain bizarre. But you know what? *Who cares?* There are billions of people in the Waking World. Why waste time dreaming about the one who can't stand you?

To beat a Meanie, the first thing you have to do is realize you're not special. Millions of people have Meanie nightmares each night. The Meanie will begin to shrink as soon as you start feeling better. Then name a person who thinks you're awesome. You only need one! Say his or her full name fifteen times in a row. By the time you've finished, your Meanie Nightmare will be so small you'll need a microscope to see it.

# FIELD NOTES

_____

_____

_____

_____

_____

_____

_____

_____

_____

_____

_____

_____

# ABOUT THE AUTHORS

JASON SEGEL used to have nightmares just like Charlie in the Nightmares! books, and just like Charlie, he's learned that the things we're most afraid of are the things that can make us strong . . . if we're brave enough to face them. Jason likes acting, writing, making music, and hanging out with his friends. Sometimes he writes movies. Sometimes he writes songs for movies. Sometimes he stars in those movies and sings those songs. You might know him from *The Muppets* and *Despicable Me*. Your parents might know him from other stuff. *Everything You Need to Know About Nightmares! and How to Defeat Them* is his fourth book for young readers. Look for the rest of the books in the Nightmares! series: *Nightmares!*; *Nightmares! The Sleepwalker Tonic*; and *Nightmares! The Lost Lullaby,* available from Delacorte Press.

KIRSTEN MILLER grew up in a small town just like the one in the Nightmares! books, minus the purple mansion. Now she lives and writes in New York City. Kirsten is the author of the acclaimed Kiki Strike books, the *New York Times* bestseller *The Eternal Ones,* and *How to Lead a Life of Crime. Everything You Need to Know About Nightmares! and How to Defeat Them* is the fourth book Kirsten has written with Jason Segel. You can visit her at kirstenmillerbooks.com or follow @bankstirregular on Twitter.